FLASH DRIVE

Joe D'Amato

This is a work of fiction. The names, characters, events, and places described herein are products of the author's imagination. A resemblance to actual events, location, or persons living or dead, is entirely coincidental.

FLASH DRIVE

First edition April 2013

Second Edition October 2018

ISBN10-06158100063

Joedamatobooks.squarespace.com

ACKNOWLEDGMENTS

Many thanks to Dorothy Binder- and Author Lou Fletcher-Murder Is Your Game. The Ohio Valley Writer's Group, The Cincinnati Writer's Project, and The Cincinnati Fiction Writers.

Chapter 1

"Extreme problems often require extreme solutions."

It was early afternoon when Lisa Turnbull wrapped her hand around the cold heel of her 9MM Glock. Noticing the bustle of activity in front of the Hotel Cincinnatian she entered quietly through the rear entrance. The gun felt heavy but reassuring.

Her thumb felt for the safety, checking its position. She thought over the plan she had put together one more time.

Passing the elevators, she arrived at the door with the red exit sign and slipped into the stairwell. When she reached the second floor, she opened the heavy door a crack and glanced up and down the corridor. Seeing no one, she walked through the empty hallway and stopped in front of room 220. *Good,* she thought, *there's a do not disturb sign on the door.*

She smiled as she thought of Joey Andronni giving her this opportunity to avenge the slapping around the last time she was with this pig.

Hank Thompson was always eager, so he'd probably be on the bed, naked, waiting for her. She tapped the door lightly with her knuckles and pushed it open with the back of her hand.

Hank's voice had a raspy depth to it. "Come on in, babe."

"I see you left the door open for me. May I use the bathroom? I'll only be a moment; I need to freshen up."

Hank asked from the bed, "Did you bring us some weed? If not, no problem. I've got a few joints. Oh, and there's a tray of assorted cheeses, mints, and olives on the desk. I bought us a bottle of Dom Perignon. Pour yourself a glass, and get that great body over here."

She knew his rod was already at attention. There was nothing like the anticipation of sex to distract the male animal from all other instincts, including caution.

Perfect.

When she got into the bathroom, she removed her jacket and brushed back her blonde hair revealing the bruise Hank inflicted the last time they were together. *She rubbed it gently. The bastard loves rough sex. He got more than he paid for and he still slapped me around. With the money I'm getting for this job I'll be able to get off the streets. Now it's his turn.*

Lisa removed a pair of gloves, from her purse, and slipped them on. She turned, and looked in the mirror, and smiled. Lisa pulled the silencer from her coat pocket and attached it onto the muzzle of the nine. She screwed it on, without a whisper of the metal-to-metal sound.

Lisa was ready. She opened the bathroom door and entered the room. It smelled of weed and cheap aftershave. Hank lay spread eagle, across a king-size bed. His naked manhood stood like the Empire State Building.

Frank Sinatra's "Come Fly With Me" filed the room.

Lisa said, "Love Frank's music, but what's with the lights on the ceiling?"

"I wanted to set a soft romantic mood for us."

"By the way, that's a nice package you've got there."

"I'm glad you like it. Why are you still in your clothes?"

She smiled. "There's little underneath. I'm not wearing a bra. I thought I'd give you a little show before we get it on."

"What's with the gloves?"

"I bought them yesterday. They go with this dress. You like them?"

Hank said, "Start with the panties. I love the cheeks of your ass. I can't wait to get my hands on them."

"This doesn't sound like the Hank who slapped me around a few weeks ago."

"Well, things have changed, haven't they?"

Lisa looked around the room. "Why did you pick this hotel? It looks like you paid a lot for it."

"Who gives a shit. The city of Cincinnati is paying for it."

Hank patted the bedspread. "Come on, Lisa, get over here."

"What's your hurry?" she asked. "You know it's better to drag this out a bit. We've got all afternoon."

"Which means I can jump you now, pour down some of that DP, reload, and jump you again."

Lisa groaned seductively. "That sounds heavenly." She walked to the wall and dimmed the lights before moving to the nightstand.

"Hey, come back here."

"You're going to need a hat for that big guy."

"You know I don't use them. Using condoms is like washing

your feet with your socks on."

She removed a black object from her handbag and flashed it for him to see.

He squinted and propped himself up against the pillow. "What's that, one of the toys you use on your Johns?"

"This is the toy I use when they can't rise to the occasion. It's long and hard. I guarantee it'll put a jolt into you."

Hank squinted in the semi-darkness, his focus moving to the black object in her hand.

She flicked the safety off and brought both hands together gripping the Glock.

"What the hell are you doing?"

"Joey Andronni is very disappointed in you, but he still sends his regards. He's sorry things didn't work out."

Hank tried to scramble backward but had no place to go. Even in the dimness of the room, Lisa could see the fear in his eyes.

"You should know a fish with its mouth closed never gets caught. And when you fuck Joey Andronni, Joey fucks back."

Lisa moved closer to the bed. "Death is like the wind, Hank. You can't see it, but you feel it when it comes."

Her dark eyes narrowed a moment, and then she squeezed the trigger.

The first round caught him in the throat, and his hands flew up to wrap around his neck. He sputtered, trying to scream, but his voice no longer worked.

She let Hank squirm a moment and then squeezed two rounds into his groin.

"Not quite the ejaculation you were expecting, was it Hank?" she smiled. "Oh well, remember, Joey what likes to say, all good things must come to an end."

She took a step forward and aimed the 9 MM point blank at his head, savoring the widening panic in his pain-filled eyes a few moments before firing the final round.

She whispered, "Go to hell."

Hank's body went tense for a second. His head snapped back. His eyes flickered like a weak electric bulb. His chest heaved, and then he was still.

Lisa glanced at the mess, on the pillow, behind his head. She walked to the wall, turned the dimmer switch, and quickly found the spent cartridges.

Lisa walked back to the bathroom searching every inch of it to make sure she forgot nothing.

The expression of shock was on Hank's face, frozen there forever. Hank's clothes lay on the floor next to the bed. She pawed through his pockets until she found his cell phone, the room key, and his wallet. She removed the cash, and placed it in her purse.

Next, she walked over to Hank's laptop computer, placed a small flash drive into a port and downloaded the device's content's.

Harry, my computer geek friend, said I should place flash drive into the laptop's port. It would only take a few minutes to download information from the computer. Then I should place the virus unit into the computer. That should wipe the hard drive clean.

When the transfer was completed, she took one more look around the room. Lisa smoothed her dress, and put on her jacket. She wedged her knuckle into the gap between the door and the jamb, and swung it open. Lisa looked back at Hank's face twisted in death and blew him a kiss. She glanced, up and down the hall, looked back at Hank, and said, "The shot in your head was for Joey. The one to your balls, you sadistic bastard, was for me."

Chapter 2

"Meet me at the Royal Cincinnatian, Jake. There were some serious fireworks at the hotel. There's a guy on the second floor with his rocks shot off."

"He's got a hole in his head and his groin looks like Swiss cheese."

"Ouch!"

*   *   *

My name is Jake Laird and I'm a trained lawyer. I had more people coming in wishing me luck than I had clients. That forced me to trade my law license for a Billy Club and join the Cincinnati Police Department.

I've been in the department for the last twenty years. I did two tours in the 'sandbox,' Iraq, and, to be honest, if it weren't for my street partner, Sam, I'd go back to practice law.

Sam Ferris is a forty-eight year old Irishman who dresses like he just got out of bed. He's losing his wavy hair and combs what's left of it with a towel. Originally from New York, he came to Cincinnati when his husband, Christopher Epstein, a dress buyer with Macy's, transferred here.

That's right, I said husband. Gay detectives on the New York police force may be the norm, but here in Cincinnati, it's as unusual as a virgin hanging out in the Playboy mansion.

When some of the boys in blue heard a gay officer had been

assigned to this division, they planned to have some fun at his expense. They backed off when they met a 240-pound six-foot-four weightlifter who bench presses 425 pounds. I only know a couple of gays. What they do in the privacy of their bedroom is their business. Me? I like the warm, soft touch of a woman.

Sam joined the Cincinnati Police force three years ago. He likes to say Mayor Bloomberg sent him to Cincinnati to keep the local hoods from stepping up the felony ladder.

Chapter 3

Another murder in a hotel in downtown Cincinnati. This one sounded like an oncoming headache. I popped a couple of aspirins and got dressed.

Three blue and white cruisers blocked off Vine Street in front of the building.

When we met Sam was wolfing down a bagel with lox and cream cheese. I can't figure out where he puts it. He eats as if he's going to the chair, yet he looks like Arnold Schwarzenegger. I'll bet he has muscles in his shit.

"I see they've already established a perimeter," I said, looking at the yellow crime tape.

"They won't need that." Sam pointed to the University Hospital ambulance.

Across the street, the local TV channels had set up their equipment using the hotel entrance as a backdrop.

When we got off the elevator, the hallway outside Room 220 was cluttered with techs from downtown and uniformed police trying to keep the hall clear.

I lingered for a moment, flashed my gold badge at the guard at the door, and stepped inside.

My eyes soaked up the flashing green and red lights flickering on the ceiling. The sound of Frank Sinatra's *Fly Me to the Moon* wafted through the room. "Will somebody turn that damn thing off?"

"You don't like Sinatra, Jake?"

"I love his music, but only with a glass of vodka in my hand, and my arms around a woman. Not in front of a guy whose crotch was blown away, and please turn off those rotating lights."

Sam asked the guard, "Where's the media set up?"

"There's a hospitality suite at the end of the hall. The press and TV are there with our people."

Harry Medford, the Crime Unit's Crew chief, was already wearing his latex gloves, so I didn't shake his hand. He and his men were wearing paper booties over their shoes. "You're going to need these," he said, giving us a pair.

Sam and I slipped them on, put on our latex gloves, and Harry handed me a wallet.

"Jake, say hello to Mr. Hank Thompson. I wonder what he was getting ready for."

I opened the wallet, and saw Mr. Thompson grinning at me from his Illinois driver's license. He was from Chicago. A Visa, an American Express, and a couple of MasterCard's were inside. It also contained three hundred dollars.

"Make sure we photograph and mark everything in the room," I told Medford.

"I think we can rule out robbery," Sam said.

"There's killing and there's a cold blooded killing. With all this blood, this one looks like the cold-blooded kind."

When you've been in law enforcement for as long as I have you'd think I'd get used to seeing things that make you sick. Before I was in homicide, I spent five years in Vice. I've seen hookers cut up so badly by pimps it would make Jack the Ripper cringe.

I knelt down and took a long hard look at the body. Thompson was short, chubby, a potbellied guy in his mid-fifties. His forehead was cracked open. The clots of blood covered his face and his pelvis. The hole in his throat looked like I could have stuck my fist through it.

Blood was everywhere. The pillow and sheets appeared as though the bed was hosed down with one of his arteries.

"You smell that? It smells like weed."

"I bet the guy was puffing on a joint before he got blown away."

"The M.E.'s office should confirm that. Check the room to see if there's any of that stuff around here so it can be used as evidence from the crime scene."

"Who's here from the Coroner's office?" I asked Medford.

I glanced back at the door, hoping Veronica Mendenhall would walk through.

"Doctor Halliday," he answered.

"What about Mendenhall?"

"I haven't seen her."

"Where's Halliday?"

"Down the hall talking to the hotel manager," Medford said. "The guy on the bed was working for the city."

"How's that?"

"He works for a Chicago auditing company that's looking into the city's finances."

"Can't the Cincinnati work on its own books?" I asked.

"The City Council hired an outside agency to keep it transparent."

"That's a joke. The guys from Chicago have their own definition of transparency. Honest officials in Chicago are as rare as white flies."

"Here," Sam said, handing me the laptop. "Maybe we can see who's on his e-mail list."

I flipped it open and pushed the ON button, slowly lighting up the screen.

Medford said. "I'll look at it in the lab and let you know if there's anything we can use on the hard drive,"

"Look for a cell phone, Harry. If this guy's got a laptop, he's got to have a blueberry, a crack berry, a dingle berry, or whatever the hell they call those things. And don't forget to take everything you find in the bathroom."

"Again you're telling me my business?" Medford complained.

"I'm sorry, Harry. What do you think was the weapon?"

"With all the blood on the headboard, the sheets, and the body, I'd say a nine or a .357. I'll know more when we dig the bullets out of Mr. Thompson, and the wall."

I asked Harry. "Didn't anyone hear the shots?"

"Probably used a silencer, and we didn't find any shells."

"I suspect they cleaned up afterward. That makes it look like a hit. What's that?" I said, pointing to a discoloration in the carpet at the foot of the bed.

"That's why I gave you those booties. And watch your step. God knows what the hell that is. There's some of it on the sheets too. Forensics can figure that out," Medford replied.

"Who found the body?" I asked, handing him the laptop

"One of the maids," Medford muttered. "You know the ones that turn down the beds and place a piece of chocolate on the pillow."

A bad feeling came over me about this one. The majority of homicides are about money or sex. This one wasn't about money; there was plenty in his wallet, so someone had another reason for Mr. Thompson's demise.

Chapter 4

While Medford's somber-faced technicians were monitoring the crime scene, I thought I'd have a few words with the chief medical examiner.

Sam asked. "Do you think it was a hit?"

"Probably, do you remember the case we worked on where the guy was found in the Ohio River?"

"Yeah, the guy was so full of bullets it's a wonder he floated."

"That was a mafia hit, Sam. I doubt if this one is. Whoever did this was really pissed at Mr. Thompson. Stay here and keep looking for that cell phone. He has to have one. The way it smelled back there, his weed stash must be somewhere in the room. As soon as you've gotten this place swept have the public relation officer update the media. And tell them to just give them a few pictures, but only from the doorway, behind the crime scene tape. I'm going down the hall to see why Doc Halliday's here and not Mendenhall."

*   *   *

Dr. Fred Halliday, head of the County's Medical Examiner's office, is known in the precinct as *'Jabba the Hutt.'* The guy is big enough to eat hay. He's so incompetent, he couldn't hit water if he fell out of a boat."

Walking down the crowded hallway, I passed a half-dozen uniformed policemen before I caught up with him.

Dr. Halliday smiled, but it wasn't a happy smile.

"You and Ferris working this case?"

I nodded. "Where's Doctor Mendenhall?"

He shrugged. "Unfortunately, there was a drive-by in Avondale. She's working that one. Mayor Bergman asked me to run this one."

I studied Halliday's face. "Mayor Bergman? How'd he find out so fast?"

"The hotel called his office. The Reds have worked out an opening day promotion with all the downtown hotels and he wants me to clear this up. He wants things to be back to normal."

I tried to keep a straight face. There had to be another reason. With the Findlay Market opening day parade, the first game was always a sellout. The Cincinnati Reds draw more flies than fans for their next home game.

"Where's the hotel manager?"

"Over there," he said, pointing toward a man pacing the hallway. "He didn't have much to tell me about the guy in 220."

"I'll make you a deal with you, Doc. I'll try not to cut up your corpses if you stay away from interrogating my witnesses."

Halliday nodded and waddled away, swaying from side to side like Charlie Chapin. I don't like the lazy bastard, but his assistant, Doctor Veronica Mendenhall, now she's another story.

Actually, Veronica runs the Hamilton County coroner's office. She has a medical degree specializing in criminal pathology from The University of Cincinnati. A board certified pathologist, she conducts the autopsies. All that and the woman's a twelve out of ten. I was hoping she'd be here instead of her boss. Hank Thompson was one lucky stiff. He would be happy to know Veronica was the last woman who worked over him. I was jealous. I dreamed about being on her like a Kodiak bear on a school of salmon.

"Call me if there's anything else I can help with," the hotel manager said after Halliday disappeared down the corridor.

I stepped in front of him and flashed my gold shield in his face.

"Detective Jake Laird, Homicide. Doctor Halliday tells me you're the hotel manager, sir."

"Yes, my name is Ira Levy. The officer who just left is a doctor?"

"He's from the coroner's office."

"I thought he was a detective."

"No, he's the guy that cuts into people like your guest in 220. Speaking of your guest down the hall, when did he check in?"

"This morning."

"I need a record of all incoming and outgoing calls made from that room after he checked in."

"Yes, sir."

"I also need to know how many keys he was given. Do you record the licenses of your guest's cars?"

"Yes, we do. We comp the customer's parking in a lot around the corner on Sixth Street. I can give you that information."

"I'll need the license number and make of his car."

"Is there anything else I can help you with?"

"Yeah. You've got surveillance cameras, right?"

"Yes, we do. They're the latest up-to-date units."

"How's that?"

"They're in color. We've got them covering all the entrances and exits."

"Thank you, Mr. Levy. I'll meet you in your office, and pick up the memory discs when I leave."

I moved down the end of the hall to the door marked EXIT and looked around for a surveillance camera. So much for the up-to-date units; there weren't any.

I decided to check the first floor.

I walked down one flight of stairs and opened the door. It led to the back of the building. There was a surveillance camera there. Its lens was pointing to the elevators. I took the elevator up and went back to the crime scene.

When I got back to the room, Medford and Halliday had already left with Mr. Thompson. Sam was on his hands and knees with his head under the bed.

"What are you doing, Sam? Still looking for a cell phone?"

He rose slowly to his feet, pushing down with his hands on his knees for leverage. He hung his head and scratched his black two-day-old facial stubble.

Sam held up a small bag of weed. "I found the guy's stash under the bed. I think we're going to have a problem with the watch commander."

"How's that?"

"I screwed up."

"What'd you do?"

"Well, Thompson's head was bowed so low the press couldn't get a photo of his face. Someone shouted for me to hold up his face so they could get at least one good shot."

I shook my head. "Don't tell me you let the press in the room?"

"No, no, they stayed behind the tape. They took their shots from the doorway."

"Oh, God," I grunted. "Tell me you're not in the picture."

There was moment of silence before the answer came. "Yeah, as soon as I gripped his chin, and held it up, the cameras went off. I screamed at them not to print any shot with me in it, but you know those bastards."

"Hell, you know better than that." I shrugged my head sympathetically. "Now we're going to have to explain to the white shirts why we're helping the press. I'll think of something to tell them. I'm sure they're gonna want to know what we have."

"The watch commander is asking questions?" Sam asked.

"Not yet, but if this guy was working on the city's finances, we're going to have the brass looking over our shoulders."

Jake

Chapter 5

I couldn't sleep. It had been three months since Carol ran off. I guess still was not used to sleeping with Maggie's furry head on my lap. Damn it; I wanted my old life back.

Until I met Carol, I toured all the bars up and down Vine Street looking for someone to have a relationship. When I met her, she told me she was tired of going out with her girlfriends and wanted to settle down. I thought we wanted the same things. Wrong again. Even though we weren't married, she managed to domesticate me. After a long day of fighting criminals on the street, having someone to come home to, a home-cooked dinner was my favorite part of the day.

I pulled the covers over my head, rolled over, and pushed my snoring dog off the bed.

*   *   *

After my morning coffee, I walked Maggie passed the Federalist-style homes in Glendale. Nothing had changed in this village in over a century. The buds on the trees were beginning to swell. I took in their sweet scent.

When we returned home, I set down Maggie's water and food for the day. No matter how much I tried, I couldn't shake the image of Hank Thompson lying on that bed.

I got into my five-year-old Mustang and headed downtown.

Traffic was light, so the drive down I-75 to Hopple Street went quickly. When I got to the Clifton section of the city, I had to fight through the University of Cincinnati traffic. I went straight to the morgue, and stuck my head in the door. The stinging smell of formaldehyde filled my nostrils.

Doctor Veronica Mendenhall stood behind her desk with a brown folder in her hands. A vase of lilacs sat on her desk. The flowers certainly helped alleviate the room's absence of décor.

She looked great. Beauty, brains, all wrapped into one neat package. Her blonde hair was pulled back in a ponytail. The soft light in her office lit up her face and made her blue eyes sparkle. She had a beautiful nose and the kind of lower lip that begged to be sucked on.

We stood there for a moment staring at each other. The prospect of working with Veronica always stimulated me.

She set the folder on her desk, pulled off her latex gloves, and dropped the gloves into the biohazard receptacle, attached to the wall, beside her desk.

Her sharp eyes twinkled.

"Hello, Jake Laird," she said. "You here to see Mr. Thompson?"

"Have you worked on him yet?"

"I just finished the prelims, but I still have to work up the report."

"Anything unusual?"

She handed me the preliminary report. "Other than the fact Mr. Thompsons's testicles look like scrambled eggs, no. Want to see the body?"

I nodded.

"He's in the fridge, follow me. He had traces of marijuana in his bloodstream. At least he was feeling relaxed before he bought it."

"He died because of the hole in his head, right?" I asked.

"Yes, but he also had a heart attack."

"Makes sense," I said, "Having a gun stuck in your face might put your heart on hold."

Veronica led me across the room to the refrigerated vault. She rolled Thompson out, uncovered him, pointed to his face, and then his groin.

"The blood on his face and groin was so thick it was difficult to remove. He looks clean now, but with all that hair on his chest and groin it took me the better part of a half hour to clean him up."

"He's had liposuction here and a facelift. He had a five-way for lunch. The combination of chili, onions, beans, and cheese on top of spaghetti isn't easy to digest. He didn't have any of the champagne you found in his room. Other than that, he's your run of the mill Viagra user."

"Viagra?"

"Yes, that's probably why he didn't have any bubbly. It doesn't work so well when you've had alcohol."

"What was the weapon?"

"I'm not sure, but by the look of the damage and all the blood, I'd say it wasn't a twenty-two."

She pointed to the hole in Thompson's forehead. "He was shot once in the head, three times in his groin, and once in the throat. The headshot took out the back of his skull and killed him instantly. From that range, the killer couldn't have missed. Oh, and toxicology said the stain mixed with the blood on the sheets was urine."

"He pissed himself?"

Veronica winked, "And so did she."

I pondered her remarks for several seconds.

"The fluid Harry scraped from the foot of the bed had female DNA. Your killer is a woman. She unloaded too. It's not unusual for someone to get so excited they empty their bladder."

"I thought only dogs did that."

"Human's do too."

"The information came back fast," I said.

"Checking the fluid you guys found on the bed, and the floor was the first thing Medford did."

"Ugh. When do you fix the time of the shooting?"

She looked back at the folder.

"Hard to tell with all this damage, but I figure sometime between three and six last evening."

"The killer had to have a lot of hate for this guy."

"You think it's a hit, Jake?" she asked as we walked back to her office.

"I do, but we don't know all the facts yet. Hits are usually one or two shots to the head. Female hitters are rare. I doubt a hitter would wet her pants. I understand you had a shooting in Avondale last night."

"Drive-by gang shooting. A nineteen-year-old kid walking along Reading Road wearing the wrong colors."

"Who's working that case?"

"Al Hoffman, District 2."

"I worked with Al on a drug case a few years ago. He's a good man."

I tried to bring something to the conversation besides my boyish charm.

"Speaking of good men, how about having lunch with me?"

"I can't," she said, "I paper bagged my lunch today."

"I don't know how you morgue guys can wrap your teeth around a ham sandwich after you've drilled holes into these stiffs."

That brought a smile to her face. A pot of coffee was steaming on the hot plate. She walked over and poured herself a cup.

"When you've had close encounters with these corpses as long as I have," she said, after taking a sip, "you get used to it."

"What about dinner? I need a Montgomery Inn fix."

She raised an eyebrow. "With you, Jake?"

"No, with Mr. Thompson over there," I said with a laugh.

She got up and leaned against the desk and looked at me. "I'd like to, Jake, but I'd better not."

"Why? I thought you loved ribs."

Veronica thought for a moment. "You know why. I'm not climbing into that state of mind Carol put you in."

She was right. I jolted back to reality.

My cell started to vibrate. I reached under my jacket and pulled it off my hip.

"Excuse me, Veronica."

Sam's voice from the other end. "Jake, we got Thompson's cell number from the carrier and verified it from his office in Chicago. The phone company gave us the numbers of everyone who called him today. The last call was at 5:18 p.m. with a 312 exchange."

"That's in Chicago. What about the earlier calls?"

"He got some from his office and a couple to his home."

"Where'd the 5:18 come from?" I asked.

"It had a Kentucky area code, 502."

"Did you trace the number?"

"Yeah, a dead end, Jake. A throwaway."

"What about the laptop?"

"Useless. The lab said the hard drive was wiped clean. They made it sick."

"Sick? What do you mean sick?"

"Someone gave it a virus."

"A virus?"

"Yeah, they used a Bleachbit."

Lisa

CHAPTER 6

Hank had it coming. He was a horny bastard. He was married with three kids and screwing me. I'm glad I got the contract to put him to sleep. Now he sleeps alone. I hope he went straight to Hell. The last time I was with him, he smacked me around. Whacking him got me even. Like Joey said, it was Hank's time to visit the Devil.

All men have it coming. Since I was sixteen, they've taken advantage of me.

None of them cared about Lisa Turnbull. They didn't care about what I wanted or needed. All they wanted was to feel me up and get into my pants.

It was my fault my life went in the wrong direction. I should have been paying more attention to what my teachers were trying to pound into my empty head.

My father left my mom right after I was born. Mom said he didn't want the responsibility of having a child and ran off with some rich broad.

My lowlife stepfather left mom a year after he moved in. He was a degenerate gambler. When he took off with another woman, my mother started her intimate relationship with the bottle. Consistently showing up drunk and late for work got her fired from the phone company. One of us had to work. I loved her, but the only thing my mother was good at was bending her elbow and lifting a glass. I had to find a way to make some money to help support the three of us. My mom, the ten-dollar-a-gallon, cheap wine, she called 'sweet red,' and me.

At sixteen, I used my breasts to make some money after school.

When you have big breasts, you take advantage of the guys who would rather see the real thing than look at a Playboy magazine.

My life down the wrong path started one afternoon when class let out. I asked Billy, the guy who sat behind me in our math class, "How would you like to get a good look at my chest?"

"Are you serious?" He asked.

"Sure I am. It will only cost you two dollars."

"Here? Now?" he asked excitedly. "I don't have any money on me."

"Then go home and get some. I'll meet you in the park behind the school in an hour."

Four-thirty that afternoon, Billy showed up with four of his friends.

I walked to the heavily wooded part of the park with the five of them close behind.

"Okay," they said in unison, "Let's see them one at a time."

I guess they figured the show would last longer if I did it one at a time.

"No. All at once or forget it. First, give me the money. Then I'll show them."

They complained at first, but 36 double Ds can be an exciting sight to teenage boys.

I collected the ten dollars, lifted my sweater, flashed, and then shook my breasts for ten seconds. Then I covered them.

They yelled in unison. "That's it?".

"Yes, five dollars more and you get to feel them."

Naturally, when the word got around the next day at school, I got dirty looks and insults from the girls and smiles from the boys. Half the juniors must have approached me. The seniors were smarter. They were always getting laid by the cheerleaders. They wanted the show for nothing.

I made seventy dollars that week, most of it over that weekend.

When word spread through the school, and I wound up in the principal's office, they suspended me.

Suspended? Bullshit. I'll show them. I quit school. That's when my mom's college dream, for me, went up in smoke. She wanted me to go to The College of New Jersey, but the closest I got to the school was the student's parking lot.

Without a high school diploma, the only jobs I qualified for were unskilled ones. You know, fast food restaurants, waiting tables, and supermarket clerks. The week after I left school my mother was caught stealing booze from a liquor store and spent thirty days in the slammer. I buried her six months later. Figures, she was the victim of a hit and run. Wouldn't you know it, the driver was drunk. She wandered into the street, and you guessed it, she got hammered. That left me alone to fend for myself. I did the waitress gig on and off for five years and then moved on to what I thought was big time.

Since I lived near the New Jersey-Pennsylvania border, I found a job serving drinks in one of the casinos on the Atlantic City boardwalk.

The revealing costume, with a low-cut top, showed off my chest. That insured me good tips. When I didn't complain about men patting my ass or brushing against my breasts, the tips were better. Some of the guests invited me up to their room for a hundred dollars an hour. Two months after I started working at the Ocean Casino, I met Carmine.

Now there was a piece of shit if there ever was.

Carmine, 'Green Eyes' Salerno, was a fast-talking, woman-chasing, connected guy from South Philly. He was a small man with a narrow, chiseled face and a trace of an Italian accent. He was highly skilled and charming. Carmine was a small-time bookie looking to get bigger. His deep green eyes instantly drew women, and I was no exception. We met at one of the crap tables where I was serving drinks.

There are two types of people looking for free drinks at a casino. There are the ones who are gambling and the ones who aren't. The casino trained us to notice the difference.

This guy, with the deep green eyes, dressed in a silk suit, was

23

a high roller.

"Here, babe," he said smiling at me as if he wanted to wolf down a delicious dessert. He tossed me a twenty-five dollar chip.

"I need a Makers Mark on the rocks."

I brushed a lock of blond hair behind my ear. "The drinks are free."

Carmine winked at me and said, "Atsa for you, babe. Remember where I am and keep the drinks coming."

Up until then, the biggest tip I ever got for getting a customer a drink was a five-dollar chip.

"What if you move to another table?"

"Then you gotta follow me."

I knew what he wanted, but I thought if he threw that kind of money around for a few drinks, there might be no limit to what he'd spend to keep me happy.

"My shift ends in an hour," I told him. "I'm not sure who will replace me."

He glanced at his watch. "When your shift ends you follow Carmine."

That night he got what he wanted. At age twenty-one I left the dump I called an apartment and never looked back. Carmine set me up in an apartment a block from the boardwalk in Atlantic City.

During the summers I spent my days waiting on the casino tables. At night, I worked on the dance floor at a gentleman's club, The Runway. Dave Seltzer, a friend of Carmine's, owned it.

Dave was a weird, wired, big redhead, always looking to get into the older dancer's pants. The degenerate bastard's favorite expression was, "I like them over forty. They don't yell, they don't swell, and they're as grateful as hell."

If you wanted to work at Dave's place, and that's where the money was, you had to sleep with him. Carmine made sure I didn't have to go that route, but horny Dave never gave up trying.

Soon Carmine worked out a deal with Dave and had me listed on the club's marquee as its headliner. Thirty-dollar lap dances and working the runway netted me better than four-hundred dollars a night. Half went to the club and the rest I had to fight to keep out of Carmine's pocket.

Most bookies have a gambling problem, and Carmine was no exception. When I tried to hold back some money the bastard smacked me around. Carmine minded my business so much there wasn't any left for me to mind. I considered leaving him, but where was I going to go? I made good money, had a place to stay, and I was the top act at the club. I had to take his bullshit.

One day in early April, Carmine finally hit it big at the tables and wanted to celebrate. Although it was a Friday, usually a busy night at the club, he got me the time off. I found out later that he, and Dave, promised the new girl, Jenna, top billing. She had blond hair, a tight ass, breast implants, and was slutty enough for both of them to get into her pants at the same time.

*   *   *

The night of April 8th, 1977 in New York turned out to be scary, but exciting. We were to have a late dinner in lower Manhattan. Carmine had to make a quick stop before we drove into town. His destination, he said, was a store in the Astoria section of Queens. He brought his black Cadillac to a halt in front of Nick Roman's candy store on 30th. Street.

"You can come inside, sweetheart," Carmine said as he helped me out of the car. "This won't take long." Carmine pointed toward the counter. "Sit over there, babe. I need to talk to my friend, Nick."

He gave Nick a high five, walked over to the newspaper rack, and thumbed through a sports magazine. When the store emptied, Carmine went to the door and flipped the open sign over to CLOSED.

"Nick, give me this week's envelope and make it quick," Carmine said with a smile. "I got a date with that gorgeous woman over there."

Nick grumbled. "This was not a good week. The ponies are still coming up from Florida, so the heavy betting at Belmont hasn't come in yet. The baseball season is getting underway. The basketball playoffs start tomorrow. The take this week was light."

Carmine smiled. The smile I've seen him use at the club when he was shaking someone down. It enabled him to lull his mark into thinking he was not a menace. "You listen to me, Nick. That story goes into the bullshit file."

Carmine glanced over at me. Then he shoved Nick back against the magazine rack. "You don't give me a light envelope, you understand? We gave you this place so you can earn. You know the program. If it is light, you make up the difference, but at the twenty percent vig."

Carmine reached into his pocket, shoved Nick across the store, and placed two .38 caliber shells on the counter. He flashed his nickel-plated revolver at him.

"You see these, Nick?" he said pointing to the shells. "If you're ever short again, a third one is going to go in your fucking head, and the Statue of Liberty will be looking down at you in New York's Harbor. You got that?"

"Carmine, please," Nick pleaded, "I've got Sal 'the Bull's' people with their hands out, too."

"You think my people give a shit about Sal the bull?"

Nick cut his complaint short when a young couple peered into the store. He went over to the door, turned the sign back over and invited them in.

With a twisted smile, Carmine said, "I'll take that lemon and lime with water now, Nick. Get a pack of *Winston Lights* for my lady friend over there."

"A pleasure," Nick said, smiling. "I'll be right with her."

Carmine grew impatient as customers began to move in and out of the store. When he finished his drink, he got up and, while motioning me to join him, said to Nick, "And you'd better make up your mind whom you're working for, and you better do it quick, or you'll have months to think about it from a fucking hospital bed."

"Sorry, babe, but I had to make this stop," Carmine said, walking out of the store. "Business is business."

Chills were running up and down my spine. It was the first time I saw Carmine use a gun to intimidate someone.

Lisa

CHAPTER 7

When we left Astoria, I asked Carmine, "Where're we going for dinner?"

"A Taste of Sicily. It's the finest restaurant in Little Italy."

"Little where?"

"You know? Down in the village."

"Oh, great. I've never been there."

The truth is I had no idea what the hell he was talking about. I didn't think there were any villages in New York City.

The restaurant stood on Mulberry Street in lower Manhattan. There was a slight drizzle when Carmine pulled into the parking lot. We entered through the side door. It was after ten and the place was all but empty. The restaurant's walls were white tiles decorated with multicolored flowers and black and white pictures of cities, villages, and the countryside of Italy. Butcher-block tables were set for two and four diners. The smell of garlic and rosemary filled the air.

As we were escorted to a table, Carmine stopped short, smiled, and nodded hello to a couple of burly men seated next to a woman with far too much makeup. Next to them sat a little girl.

"That's Angelo *'pazzo'* Santucci, his sister, and her daughter," Carmine whispered, smiling at the man seated at the center of the table.

Pazzo, Carmine explained, "is the Italian slang for crazy. The big guy next to Angelo is 'Fat Freddie.' Freddie used to be a bouncer in the club across the street."

"Angelo's crazy?" I asked.

"Some say he acts crazy."

Fat Freddie drew a bead on us through the smoke of his nasty smelly cigar.

After we were seated I asked Carmine what I should order.

"Get the broiled shrimp and *scungilli*. It's served with the best crusty bread in Little Italy."

Carmine ordered a bottle of white wine. I told him I wanted red, but Carmine barked at me. "What's wrong with you? You order white with fish, red wine with meat. Order white. We're in a fucking fish restaurant."

The people at Santucci's table were laughing and seemed to be in a festive mood.

Santucci got up, removed his jacket, and headed for the Men's Room.

When the waiter brought the wine, a tall, slender man in a plaid sport coat stepped quietly through the side door. With his back to Carmine, he pulled out a handgun and blasted away in the direction of the man Carmine called, 'Fat Freddie'.

The fat man pushed over the table using it as a shield. Santucci's sister and her daughter ducked behind it. Carmine grabbed my arm and yanked me to the floor. Every nerve in my body went on alert. Santucci was coming back to the table, heard the gunfire, and started screaming.

He ran at top speed toward the front door. That move probably saved the lives of the woman and the little girl.

The man in the plaid coat stopped firing at Fat Freddie and blasted away at Santucci as though he was a target at a firing range. That's when I stood up and saw the first three shots ripping holes in the back of Santucci's white shirt.

I took a heart-jolting breath. Santucci staggered through the glass front door and fell onto the fender of a black Cadillac. The gunman winked at me and smiled. Santucci's sister pushed her way passed me and headed for her brother. My *'hero,'* Carmine, was still lying on the floor with his hands covering his head. The gunman stopped shooting the moment Santucci went out the front door. He backed out the side door, and disappeared.

Fat Freddie raced by me and ran out the side door into the street. I watched through the glass door as he fired off five shots at the car speeding away. He came back into the restaurant, vaulted the clam bar, and ran into the kitchen.

He was screaming at the cook loud enough to be heard in New Jersey.

He yelled, "If I find out any you had anything to do with this, I'll cut your fucking throat and feed you to my dogs."

Excited, I felt warmth surging through my body. I ran to the front of the restaurant. Out on the curb, Angelo's sister was wailing as she held her brother's head in her lap.

The gunshots must have attracted the attention of a black and white police cruiser. Seeing the car, Fat Freddie reached behind his coat and threw his gun into the street.

The two cops stuffed Santucci into the back seat and sped up Mulberry Street.

Suddenly I felt warm between my legs. I peed my panties.

Chapter 8

State House in Columbus, Ohio

Ten a.m. and State Senator Pete Reese's chief of staff, Harriet Teplitsky, was in the large, paneled outer office, glaring at the grandfather clock.

The Senator walked down the hall and stepped into his outer office.

Reese was a big man with a tight end's build under a dark grey Brooks Brothers suit. He wore a finely tailored light blue shirt and a perfectly knotted red tie.

Harriet, a heavy-set woman in her fifties, wore a plain black sweater over a white collared shirt. Holding papers in one hand, she waved them in front of the Senator.

"You've got a 10:30 meeting with the speaker," she prompted Reese.

"The morning calls are on your desk."

"Morning, Harriet."

Harriet grinned and nodded. "Good morning, sir. I've answered all the calls I could. Mr. Morgan called three times. I asked if there was something I could help him with, but he said it was pertaining to your trip to Thailand with the Ohio State Buddhism Society and you'd handle it."

Reese smiled, waved hello to the rest of his staff, and then headed for his office.

Harriet said, "Give me a minute. I'll bring you the papers that need your signature. Would you like some coffee?"

"Yes, please, Harriet. And tell Speaker Bacon I must meet with a constituent. I'll be a bit late."

A few minutes later she returned with the coffee. Reese looked up from the papers and said, "Thank you."

"You're welcome. Is there anything else, senator?" she asked.

"No, please hold my calls." He held up a stack of papers an inch thick. "I'll bring these out when I'm done looking them over."

Reese, waiting until the door had closed, nervously drummed his fingers on his desk. He reached down, unlocked the bottom drawer, and pulled it open. He removed two pills from a red leather bag and a cell phone.

Thank God, this cell is secure.

From a red bag, he removed a sweet-smelling red/orange pill, popped it in his mouth, and washed it down with a sip of coffee. He placed the bag back in the drawer.

This Yaba is going to keep me going all day.

He placed the phone in front of him and tapped in a number.

"Yeah," snapped the voice from the other end.

"It's me, Jerry."

"Where in the hell have you been, Pete? I've been trying to get you all morning. Our friend, Thompson, is gone."

"I know. Our man in Cincinnati called me late last night," Reese replied. "We may have a problem."

"What kind of problem?"

Reese's voice dropped to a whisper. "The killer drained his laptop."

"For Christ's sake, Pete. I hope you're not going to tell me he had our Yaba business records on his computer."

"He wouldn't have all that shit on the computer, would he?" Reese asked.

"How the hell would I know?" Jerry said. "We have no idea what was on that computer. If he kept any of our information on the damn thing, we're all going to jail until we're old and grey. Our man on the hill, with the help of our friend in New York, has been raiding union funds to finance our drug deals. If the drug operation is on the hard drive we're in deep shit."

"Maybe there's nothing about our operation on it," Reese replied.

"I hope you're right. The police think it was just a hooker that he was screwing. The woman probably has no idea what she's got."

Jerry asked, as gently as he could manage. "Does our friend in New York know?"

"I don't think so, but now is not the time to talk to him. My people tell me he's got shingles. I understand he's had it for months."

"Ouch, you're right. I wouldn't want to be around him."

"Let's hope it was his idea to hit Thompson and have the woman drain his computer," Jerry said.

"For what reason?"

"Thompson was Morrison's man. Our guy in New York doesn't trust Senator Morrison. He wants one of his own men stealing from the unions."

"Well, I hope Thompson's computer was filled with porno and poker games."

"But if it's not, it won't matter to the guy in New York. The idea that it's a woman won't mean shit to him. What do I tell him?" Jerry asked.

"Don't be surprised if he's involved, but don't tell him anything until he asks. Especially in his condition."

Jerry said, "Oh, no. Are you out of your mind? I'm not going that route. He wants to hear bad news immediately."

"Well, then tell him we have a man inside the investigation. As soon as I get a name or a lead we'll pass it along."

"What the hell was Hank doing with a hooker?"

"Showing her his slide rule, I guess." Reese laughed at his own joke.

"How the hell should I know? But I do know one thing. Whether there's something on it or not, I wouldn't want to be in her shoes. Unless, of course, our friend in New York put her up to it."

Reese pushed his coffee aside and tapped a *Winston Light* from its pack.

"I'm sure the guy from Chicago will have his people looking for her. Add to that, the Cincinnati police are hunting her down. She'd better turn that thing over to our friend in New York. I wouldn't want his people chasing me," Reese snapped. He started to light the cigarette and stopped.

"If the guy in New York put her up to this, he wanted to see what was on Thompson's computer. My guess is he told her not to look at it."

"And if she did?" Reese asked.

"Then she better hope the Cincinnati cops get to her first."

"No, Pete, if the cops get to her first they're certain to see what was on that hard drive."

"What the hell does that matter?"

"Nothing," answered Reese. "If she's seen what was on it, New York's going to want to have her whacked."

"And if he put her up to it?"

"I don't think he wants a hitter looking into his business. Either way, the woman is toast. Our friend in New York doesn't like loose ends."

Jake

Chapter 9

Thanks to my barber, I was having a bad hair day. I wish he'd spend more time cutting my hair than talking. I bet he could talk under water.

Sam can't get through the day without a taste of New York. We don't have subways in Cincinnati. That means a little slice of New York is a corned beef or pastrami sandwich on rye, a cream soda, a couple of dill pickles, and something Sam calls a potato knish. I drove my Mustang to Izzy's, the Jewish deli on Main Street, and picked up his New York fix.

I got a Reuben and some coleslaw for me. I stopped by Starbucks for their cup of the day, hazelnut. I can't believe I pay three dollars for a sweet-smelling cup of coffee.

Sam was sitting in his grey cubicle shuffling through some paperwork. He read a slip of paper, reread it, crumpled it up, and threw it in his basket.

Information regarding a handful of hotel killings started coming in from the cities to which we sent communiqués. There had been a few hotel murders, but none with this M.O.

Sam already started to gather evidence we got at the Cincinnatian. The whiteboard was set up. Pinned to it were several strands of red hair, a small bag of marijuana, and a piece of the stained bed sheet. We also had Mr. Thompson's death picture, his hairpiece, and his wallet.

"Here's your lunch, Sam. By the way, the killer was a woman."

"How do you know that, Tracy?"

"Medford tested the fluid he found in front of the bed. The DNA tested female. It was urine."

"And the fluid on the sheets?" He asked pointing to the piece of sheet on the whiteboard.

"Also urine," I answered. "It was Thompson's."

"They took a pee-pee together?" Sam laughed. "I bet he had an accordion."

"An accordion?"

Sam chuckled again. "A hard-on. We, gays, prefer a visual description."

"Medford's men lifted a lot of partial prints from the room," Sam said. "The maids and the maintenance man. But they're unusable." He paused, pointing to the whiteboard. "The strand of red hair found in the bathroom came from a wig."

"How do we know it was left there yesterday?"

"We don't," Sam, replied. "You know the procedure. Medford's men found it on the bathroom floor, so they bagged it."

I sank down into the chair behind my desk, flipped the lid off the overpriced coffee, poured in a couple of packs of sugar, and took a sip.

Medford dusted the bottle of Dom Perignon found on the desk. Thompson's, along with another set of partials, were on it. The lack of information we had was disappointing, but I wasn't surprised. This killer was careful. But, as in all homicides, she probably made a mistake, and we were going to find it.

Despite intensive interviews with the people from the front desk on duty yesterday, the maids, the maintenance men, and the hotel manager, nobody remembered seeing anyone on the second floor between 5 and 7 p.m.

I knew sooner or later we'd hear from the white shirts. Phil Westrope strode out of his office, a cup of coffee in his hands, looking depressed. He pointed to his office and invited Sam and me to close the door behind us. Phil told us to sit. I remained standing. I could feel his riot act coming, and I didn't want him looming over me. That's when he waved the *Cincinnati Enquirer* in my face.

The boldface headline above the fold read,

AUDITOR SHOT AT THE CINCINNATIAN HOTEL

Phil is the second in command for this precinct. You can pretty much form an opinion about Phil in the first thirty seconds you spend with him. He's perfect for his job. Ed Cohen, the watch commander, runs his office as though it were a military unit. He uses Phil to runs errands. Phil likes to think he's a liaison between Cohen's men, the press, and the brass upstairs. Phil graduated from the University of Dayton with a criminal justice degree but has never been on the job. I think Phil's mom dropped him on his head when he was a baby. Sam says she did it on purpose. Phil was the boss's man, so I better not piss on his pants.

"Commander Cohen wants to know what you've got."

I slumped into a chair. "Right now, not much. We think Thompson had a go-round with a hooker or there's a chance it was a hit. We're casting a wide net. We've sent out wires to Columbus, Cleveland, Indy, Frankfort, Louisville, and Chicago, to see if they had unsolved shootings with this M.O. But, so far, nothing."

Phil had a unique gift of saying exactly what everyone was hoping he wouldn't say.

"And that's it, Jake? Cohen's giving me a rash," Phil said, scratching his arm. "This is bullshit, and you know it. The Chamber of Commerce and the mayor think the front-page story on this rag is going to scare the tourists away."

I took a sip of my coffee and wiped my mouth.

"What tourists? Cincinnati doesn't have tourists," I said. "Let's face it. Mayor Bergman is afraid the hotel business, like everything else, will go across the river to northern Kentucky."

Phil took a sip of his coffee, frowned, and lapsed into his speech-making mode.

"Jake, this has the boss's full attention. He's got the mayor's office all over him. Since all rivers of shit run downhill, it has already passed through me, and it's heading straight for you. He's got a stack of messages from all the local TV stations and their anchors. They're screaming for interviews. What do I tell them?"

"Feed them bullshit. You can buy any of these media clowns with a steak. How the hell do I know? You're the go-between. That's your department. Tell them a jealous woman decided to give the guy her version of a vasectomy."

Phil rolled his eyes, blew on his coffee, took a sip, and said. "I understand he got a phone call just before he got blown away." Phil shifted his gaze to Sam and back to me.

"Good, then you have something. Why the hell didn't you tell me? You guys are digging yourselves a hole here, and when you dig the hole too deep, you have to eat the dirt."

"Phil, do you want me to speak any slower? I don't know any simpler words."

Phil asked, "And that's it?"

"We're checking every wine shop, on both sides of the river, to see if any of them remember selling Dom Perignon to the victim." Phil's voice was, and I could see he was losing his patience.

"Come on, Jake, no more games. How the hell is that going to help?"

I looked up at the ceiling, knowing above the ceiling was the roof. Above the roof was the sky, and somewhere in the air was the power that could help me deal with Phil.

"Phil, you're not going to find a hundred and a thirty-dollar bottle of champagne in your neighborhood Kroger. All those liquor stores have surveillance cameras. Maybe he wasn't alone when he bought it."

I didn't have the time or the inclination to get into a battle of words with him. I got on my feet, trying to come up with anything I could say that would get him to throw us out of his office.

"What's the matter with you, Phil? We could argue until Jerry Springer becomes president. If you don't like what you see, don't look."

Phil's eyes narrowed. He was probably trying to figure out whether he could trust me.

"Go over and take a look at the whiteboard; it's practically empty," I said, trying to ignore him. "You're the boss, Phil. I'll give you whatever we find when we find it."

"Okay," he said, standing, and throwing up his hands.

"We gave this case to you a few days ago, and we need it to come to an end."

He looked down and pointed to my new shoes. "Those shoes will never get broken in if you sit around in my office."

I gave him a thumb up, and he repaid me by pointing to the door and throwing us out of his office.

*   *   *

"Why didn't you tell him it was a woman?" Sam asked.

"I don't want to tell him anything until we see what's on the surveillance tapes Medford has. Let's wait until he gets here."

"By the way, I understand Thompson's wife doesn't want the body sent to Chicago," Sam said.

"Why?"

"She said she doesn't want the bastard, as she puts it, anywhere near her, alive or dead."

"Here comes Medford," Sam said.

Harry Medford walked into the office with some discs in his hand and a laptop under his arm.

Medford said, "I was right. My guess is she has uploaded the files from the laptop, and then downloaded a virus that wiped the hard drive clean. I isolated the video from the lobby and the one from the back door. We caught a break here. They're in color. The time appeared on the lower left side of the frame."

Medford loaded a disc into the computer and attached a connection to the large screen hanging on the wall.

After a short struggle with the DVD player, Medford got it to play. We watched as he pointed out the time code on the lower corner of the surveillance disc.

"This first one is the back door," Medford said. "This frame was taken at 5:09 p.m."

"Speed that up to about 5:20."

"I've already looked at this disc. What you want to see appears at 5:24."

Then I saw something that made my heart jump.

"There she is. Freeze that."

I pulled my chair closer to the monitor.

The frame was filled with a tall blonde, looking away from the camera as she walked past the elevators. She was dressed in a red jacket and carried a large purse tucked under her arm.

"What do you have after 5:24?"

"Nothing, there were a couple of kids getting on the elevator at 5:27."

"What's that dark mark on her leg?"

"Some smudge, but we'll get a better look at it when we blow it up in the lab."

"And that's it?" I asked.

"There's a worker filling the vending machine at 5:48. No one passes that camera again until 5:59," Medford explained.

"What about the camera in the lobby?"

"Ah, now that's a different story, Jake, and you're not going to like what you see."

I looked at him, trying to figure out where he was heading. Medford slipped in another disc.

"This frame recorded 5:40," he said, freezing the image.

I asked Medford to zoom in on the woman walking alone. The frame showed a tall blonde-headed woman, in a red coat, walking toward the front entrance. She was carrying a large black bag; her face turned away from the front desk.

Sam's eyes widened, and his mouth fell open. "The black bag, that's a Barneys shopping bag."

"Never heard of it, Sam."

"It's a high price clothing store in New York."

Medford shouted, swaying as though he was on a rolling ship.

"It's her!"

"Harry, switch back to the back door video," I said.

My heart danced with glee. "There it is, but in this video, the handbag is folded and tucked under her arm."

I could hear a note of excitement in Medford's voice. "Now, in the front door video, the bag is bulging."

I'll bet she's carrying the red coat in it along with the gun, and

the cell phone in the black bag," I said. "She came in with a coat, but left in a jacket. S
he's looking away from the camera." A surge rippled through me. "Turn, bitch, damn it, turn."

And the woman did. She stopped and raised her left hand to cover the side of her face.

"She's giving you the finger, Jake."

Memories of Carol running off with Chuck drifted into my head. I pushed a smile to my lips.

This is the second woman who had told me to fuck off in the last six months.

"Sam, call Phil. Tell him the killer's a woman. Do me a favor and don't tell him she flipped us the bird."

Jake

Chapter 10

I awoke immediately when the phone, ringing at my bedside, jolted me out of a sound sleep. It pulled me out of a dream I didn't want to leave. Chuck, my neighbor, was on the business end of my wedge. I wanted to shove the club, shaft and all, up his ass.

I opened my eyes and grabbed the phone and fumbled it to my face.

"It's Carol. Are you sleeping?"

Oh no, not her, when I was enjoying the chase. What the hell does she want? She stuck the knife in me five months ago, and now she wants to twist it?

"I'm trying to sleep. What the hell do you want?"

"We need to talk."

I looked at the digital clock on the nightstand. "It's midnight, Carol. Maggie is fine. I just got to bed, and I'm running on empty. I was in court all day, and my shift starts at seven in the morning. Can't this wait?"

"No," she said. "We need to talk."

"Where are you?" I was hoping she'd say Australia, but no such luck.

"I'm in the driveway. Can I come in?"

"No, leave me alone and go back to your lover."

I swung my feet to the floor and sat up trying to concentrate on something other than Carol's voice. Right now, it was Maggie, my snoring dog.

I met Carol, two years ago, unexpectedly, in a bar on Vine Street. It was as if I'd gotten a gift from heaven. The attraction was strong and mutual. We loved each other's company. We laughed, danced, ate pizza, and drank beer all night. We had sex and fell asleep in each other's arms feeling content. Now I wake up with a snoring dog.

What was I supposed to do? I hurt inside. Although her leaving felt like she'd taken a razor to my heart, I still missed her. This call was only the second one in five months. The first time she'd forgotten her Ferragamos.

Maggie started barking at whatever dog's bark at when you're on the phone.

"Stop, Maggie, stop. I can't hear."

Maggie is a lab-collie mix. She barks louder than my ex, Carol. Like all dogs, she's a good, loyal companion, who's slept on my bed ever since my other not-so-loyal partner ran off to find herself. She found herself in my neighbor, Chuck's, bed.

There wasn't a custody battle over Maggie. Carol would have lost. I loved that dog much more than I ever loved the woman who left me. Contrary to popular belief, no one showed up at my door with a casserole.

"What do you want now, Carol? My Cincinnati Reds jacket to give to Chuck?"

"I want to talk about us."

"Us?" I stumbled from the bed and glanced out the bedroom window. "There *is* no us." She was sitting in her car, looking up at me.

I shook my head no, but she stepped out of her car.

"I brought us coffee. I'm coming up."

She can have the coffee. I hope I still have plenty of Vodka in the fridge.

Usually, Carol was a quick study. I couldn't tell why she was here. I didn't want to talk to her, but I knew that deep inside I was happy to see her.

I could see her walking toward the porch steps.

The last thing I needed was to have her pounding on the door, waking up my neighbors. I threw the phone on the bed, hurried through the living room, and unlocked the front door. I looked at the back door wishing I could escape and leave her alone with Maggie. That wouldn't work. When she left, she'd probably take the dog with her.

She fluttered in, enveloped in her Tommy Girl perfume. "No hug? No kiss hello?"

My lips wanted to move, I wanted to say something, but couldn't. I looked at Carol, tried to flash a smile, and turned away. She knows how to push the right buttons.

Maggie raced into the living room, wagging her tail, scratching her way on the hardwood floor to Carol, sticking her wet nose where it didn't belong, the turncoat.

I wish someone greeted me that way.

Carol knelt, massaging Maggie's ears. "I missed you too," she said, looking at me. "How are you?"

I turned away. I couldn't make eye contact.

She said it agan. "How are you?"

"I heard you the first time."

"I only wanted to know how you were."

"How in the hell do you think I am?"

"You look like hell. When was the last time you slept?"

I yawned and mumbled. "A few minutes ago, thanks to you. What the hell are you doing here? What do you want?"

She frowned. "I miss you."

I closed my eyes, forcing a deep breath.

"Do you remember what I did with my keys two years ago?"

"Yes. You showed me the key to the garage."

"And the second key?"

"You told me it was for the back door."

"And the third?"

"You said the front door, and they're all yours."

"Well, you gave them back to me five months ago and left." She reached out to me, but I pulled away. "Jake, I..."

"What did Chuck do? Go back to his wife?"

"No, I wanted to come home to you and Maggie."

"Look, Carol, I need to get back to sleep. I'm bone tired, and my ass is dragging. I'm working on a tough case."

She walked into the kitchen and placed a bag on the table. "I brought us some coffee, and some of your favorites from *Dunkin Donuts*," she said, opening the cabinet. "I hope the cups are in the same place."

I looked away and went to the fridge. "Yeah, and so is the vodka."

I removed the bottle of *Absolut* from the freezer and poured myself a stiff drink. Wrapping my hand around the glass, I drained it and then poured myself another.

"For God's sake, Carol, why the hell are you here?"

Her voice was warm and seductive "You're not listening, Jake. I want us to be together again."

She paused in the doorway before sitting down so that I could see her body backlit by the light behind her. "I should never have left," she continued. She popped the lid from the coffee and poured herself a cup.

"Do you know how it feels watching the woman you love pack her bags, and drive off with your neighbor? I haven't even begun to breathe right yet."

She started to cry. Carol took the edge of her dress and brought it to her wet eyes exposing her long slender legs. She knew what she was doing, and so did I.

Carol slowly wiped away the tears and set the hem of her dress down to the middle of her thighs.

"You come here after five months," I paused, glaring at her, "and you want me to forget what happened between you and Chuck? What the hell do you want?"

She stared at me over her coffee. "I want your hands all over me. I want you."

"Yeah, you wanted me right up until the moment you walked out."

She didn't answer me. Her eyes said it all.

My head was spinning. I was thinking of what we'd had together and how long it'd been since I'd made love to a woman.

She reached for my hand and placed it between her soft thighs. Deep inside me, I wanted her. I couldn't pull away.

"Look, Jake, I made a mistake," she said with a tear in her eye. Her thighs parted, and I moved my hand closer to her warmth.

She said quietly, "At least let's lie together again. I need you."

I saw a hidden side of Carol I hadn't seen the two years we lived together. I shook my head to clear my mind; I stood up and tried to walk away. I wanted to kiss the breath right out of her.

She got up and stood in the corner of the room near the bedroom door. Even though the dim light, I could see the sadness in her eyes.

Carol opened the door and stepped into the bedroom, but I didn't move.

"Come here," she said in a low voice, pulling me toward her. She rubbed her breasts against my arm.

We moved toward the bed, and Carol pulled the sheets aside. She slipped off her shoes, crisscrossed her hands, and removed her dress.

"Are you afraid of catching a cold? Here, let me take off these pajamas."

She ran her fingers over my chest, undid the strings of my pajama bottoms, and let them drop to the floor. Every part of me tingled. What the hell was I doing?

I swung my arm around Carol's waist and kissed her lips. Her tongue darted through my mouth. I began to breathe loudly. I just wanted to smell her. Hold her. I begged my heart to stop beating so swiftly.

I drew her next to me. I could feel the heat of her body next to mine. Our bodies became one.

And then my fucking cell went off.

I turned toward the ringing sound, but Carol pushed me back on the bed.

"Let it ring, baby. Come here."

"I can't, Carol. It's Sam. He's the only one who would call me this early in the morning."

"Then if it's Sam, don't answer it."

Carol reached over to me. Her nails were on my shoulders, and she was softly running them down my back.

"Come here. I want you inside me."

"I've got to answer this. If it's Sam, it's business."

"If the son of a bitch were here I'd rip his heart out. For Christ's sake, Jake, let it ring!"

I sat upright, shaking my head, trying to figure out why this was happening.

"Nothing has changed, has it?" she said. "Your job, always your fucking job."

I tried to ignore her, nails on my back and all.

There's got to be something wrong with me. I've got a beautiful woman breathing heavily next to me. I haven't gotten laid in six months, and I'm answering the fucking phone.

I reached over to the bed. Grabbed the vibrating cell that looked like a dancing light bulb. "Yeah, Sam, what the hell do you want?"

I could feel Carol's eyes digging holes in my back. Frustrated, she got up, wrapped the sheet around her, stomped into the bathroom, and slammed the door.

"Do you know what time it is, Sam? When do you sleep?"

"I'll have plenty of time to sleep when I sleep alone."

Sam sounded as though he'd spent the last year on the moon. "Did I interrupt something?"

"Yes, I had a wet dream that was actually happening."

"You were getting lucky?"

"Yes, but thanks to you, not now. Hold on."

Carol rushed out of the bathroom like an F-16 lifting off the runway. She stopped, bent down, and picked up her dress.

"The mood's gone, Jake. Be sure to thank your *real* partner."
There goes that partner bullshit again.

"Carol, wait."

"Goodbye, Jake," she screamed back in mock fury and laughed. "Believe me, wherever you're going will never be as good as where you could have been."

Jake
Chapter 11

"Meet me at the Sleep-Inn in Clifton. It looks like Thompson's killer struck again."

The Sleep-Inn, now that's a joke. In the motel business, the Sleep-Inn Motel falls into the category of a quick-sheet joint. Even with the thirty-nine dollar-a-night specials, no one sleeps there. In fact, no one spends more than an hour there, except maybe the bedbugs. The neighborhood looks like the one Jerry Springer gets his audience from. Pimps and perverts cruise place like sharks.

The hookers rent the dump by the hour. They get the bed ready for a roll in the hay, hope their johns get off in record time, and they're out the door looking for the next love of their life.

But with this john it was different. The killer didn't wait to send him to his reward in the room. He was sent there from the parking lot.

*   *   *

I threw on my clothes and slipped into my Mustang. It was a little after 1:30 a.m. when I pulled off I-75 and onto Hopple Street. When I got to the motel, Sam was waiting for me standing a few feet from a black 725 BMW. He was holding a Coke in one hand wolfing down a burrito from the all-night Taco Bell across from the motel.

The parking lot was empty except for two Cincinnati police cruisers, and the M.E. wagon parked alongside the cruisers. No doubt when they pulled up the ladies of the night, working the four corners, scattered like roaches racing across a kitchen table.

Thank you, Lord, the M.E.'s van's here. I should have figured Veronica would be working the case.

"I was putting in some overtime when I got the call," Sam explained.

"The M.E. asked me to contact you. I knew you'd be glad to see her."

I shook my head and breathed in the first fresh air I pulled in all day.

"I think she likes you."

Sam watched his words sink in.

"What makes you say that?"

"She asked me not to tell you, but she wanted to know if you're over Carol and involved with anyone."

"She asked you that?"

"It looks like she's hitting on you."

Both of the BMW's front doors were open, and Veronica was working on the victim on the passenger's side. She smiled as Sam, and I approached the car. I looked through the open door on the driver's side. It seemed like déjà vu all over again. It was a nauseating sight. The guy looked like road-kill. He was lying on his back, face up; eyes wide open, staring at the ceiling of the car. The space between his waist and the top of his thighs was covered with blood. His shorts were pulled down below his knees. The hole on the side of his head had caused a pool of blood on the leather front seat. They found four shell casings on the pavement on the driver's side of the car.

"Why do you suppose she blew his rocks, his ass, and his head off, Jake?"

I closed my eyes hoping the bloody image would go away.
Sam shrugged. "Maybe the killer is making it up as she goes along."

"She? What makes you think it's the same person that mutilated that Thompson guy? You think this a copycat?"

Sam said, "Maybe, but whoever did this left the shell casings. Maybe the Vic was sitting in his car holding his Johnson then the killer shoots him in the head."

"Then, they roll him over, and shoots him in his rear end?"

Sam said, "Yeah, they roll him over, pull down his shorts, and fires away."

"I wonder why he had his Johnson in his hands." I thought for a moment. Maybe he was getting ready for a bj."

"Let's wait until the people back at the lab give us their reports."

I shoved my hands into my pants pockets and looked at Sam. "Have a heart here. The guy's dead, and he probably has a family."

Sam's voice grew defensive. "He should have been home tucking his kids in bed or making love to his wife instead of a hooker. Where's your sense of humor?"

My eyes shifted to Veronica, who was coming around to our side of the BMW. Her hips swayed slowly from side to side. I couldn't take my eyes off of her. For a few seconds, a tingle of satisfaction rushed through me.

She wore an open white lab jacket over tight tee shirt and jeans that accented those great legs of hers.

If she's trying to turn me on, she's succeeding.

I looked across the empty parking lot in the direction of the motel's office.

I pulled Sam aside. "Do me a favor, Sam. Talk to the manager of this dump. I need to speak to Doctor Mendenhall alone."

Sam said, walking away. "Now you're talking. You haven't had any for a while, so you want to work on Mendenhall? Remember, to get *over* someone you have to have someone under you."

I was silent for a moment. "You're sick, Sam. Knock it off. My ass is worn out. I'm tired, cranky, and hungry. Between you and Carol I'd like to lie down on my front lawn and pull the grass over me."

Veronica walked up to me as though she was about to fill me in on the stiff lying in the car.

"Hi, Jake, we have to stop meeting like this. I tried to call you but got no answer. It's too late tonight, but I'd like to take you up on that dinner invitation."

"With me?" I asked.

Veronica wrinkled her nose. "No, detective, with the guy in the BMW."

"When?" I said, eagerly.

"I'm off next Wednesday night."

Thank you, God.

I thought for a moment and said deadpan.

"Let's see." Looking at the schedule on my notepad. I'm working the day shift next week. "The Gods have willed it. I think I can fit you in. I'm off that night too."

She gave me a bright smile. "Then Wednesday it is, but no ribs."

"But I thought you liked the Montgomery Inn."

"I do, but not on our first date. It's too busy, too noisy," she whispered. "Jake, you've got to watch your cholesterol."

I love a woman who cares about my health.

I closed my eyes, taking in a deep breath. "How about the Grand Finale? It's a dollar a breath, but worth every penny," I said.

She flashed those blue eyes at me. "You live near there, don't you?"

"Yes," I said, trying to act nonchalant.

"Are you trying to get me to your place for a drink after dinner?"

"The thought had entered my mind."

"We'll see. Eight o'clock?"

"Eight it is."

I quickly changed the subject. "What do you figure was the time of this killing?"

"I'd say between nine or ten."

"Same weapon used on the guy in the Cincinnatian?"

"I just dig them out," she said. "Medford's people figure that out. I'll send the shells over to them. It will be in my report."

"Have you seen the picture Medford's men took from the surveillance tape?"

"No," I admitted.

She shook her head. "Where've you been all night?"

I should have been with you.

I held up my hand. "Scout's honor, I haven't seen any picture. I was in court all day."

"How'd you miss it? Medford's people were able to blow up what they first thought was a dirt smudge on her left leg."

I looked at her for a moment. The last thing I wanted to do was talk shop. I keep wondering, what was a woman who looked like this doing slicing into dead bodies.

Veronica stepped back, reached into her coat pocket, and pulled out a photograph.

"Oh, by the way, Medford had the image, which looked like a smudge, magnified from the disc, and passed the picture along to everyone in the department."

"The whole department?"

"Yeah," she said. "Medford wasn't sure what it meant and hoped someone would know."

I paused trying to remember if my cell went off before Sam called. "I had my cell on silent today while I was in court. I must not have turned it on when I got back home."

"Here it is. It's a little rough. Medford thinks it looks like the Medusa, she paused, with three legs.

I looked at the picture until blood came out of my eyes. "Is this the smudge that was on Thompson's killer's leg?"

Sam was wandering toward the Cincinnati policemen, but I motioned him over to us.

I said, handing the picture to him. "Look at this, Sam, Medford found it on the hotel's surveillance disc."

Sam took his readers from his breast pocket, set them on his nose, and stared at the photo.

"Oh yeah, I've seen one of these before."

"Where?" I asked.

"I was on a case in the Bronx, no, Manhattan. Oh, yeah," he said, "It looks like a Trinacria."

I scratched my head and shot him a puzzled look. "A what?"

"A Trinacria."

"What's a Trinacria? I'd hate to poke around in your sick mind. God only knows what I'd find in it."

"The symbol of Sicily," he said, running his hand through his thinning hair.

"I didn't know you were into that crap. Maybe it was done in

Chicago or L.A.," I said.

"I've never been in L.A. or Chicago, but I worked in New York, remember? Half the wise guys in Little Italy who have a Sicilian background relate to this figure."

"Why the legs?" I asked.

"It signifies the shape of Sicily, a triangle."

"What do Sicily and Medusa have in common?"

Veronica said, "Medusa was banished there."

"It's a perfect symbol for the Sicilian wise guys," Sam said, laughing.

"Both turn your tushie to stone if you look at them funny."

"You're right, Veronica," I said. "This looks like our first real lead."

Veronica looked at Sam and me. "All you guys have to do now is find out what tattoo place around here does this kind of work."

"Hey wait a minute, in the surveillance tape, the killer was carrying a Barneys the clothing store in mid-town Manhattan."

A glimmer came to Sam's eyes. "You're not going to find this kind of tattoo in this town."

"Where then?" I asked.

"Between the Barneys bag, and the tattoo, it looks like I'm going home for a while."

"How's that?"

"How many people are working on this investigation?"
I shrugged. "Just the two of us."

"We're going to ask Cohen if we can take this investigation to Manhattan. Not Chicago or L.A., but the Big Apple."

Jake
Chapter 12

If our District Commander Ed Cohen, had an ounce of grey matter, he'd tell Sam and me to get back to work and let the New York police handle the search for the tattoo artist.

That's not a fair statement, though. Sam can be very persuasive. My partner's main argument was that given the probable age of the killer, and the subject matter of the tattoo, it was a good bet that she had the work done in New York. Sam had worked in lower Manhattan for fifteen years. If she was a hooker, there was a chance that he might even know her.

Working the streets of New York was the reason Sam became a detective. He loved the action, understood the wise guy's mentality, and craved the level of power that law enforcement displayed.

Since Thompson was murdered in our jurisdiction, we should be the ones who follow this lead.

Sam told Commander Cohen. "I worked a case in New York a few years back when a wise guy worked over a tattoo artist. The kind of sketches he had on his bench was the one we saw on our killer."

"I don't want any of your bullshit, Ferris." Cohen asked, "What makes you think that guy has anything to do with the woman we're looking for?"

"I know some of the people in the tattoo business. These dudes are artists. They pride themselves on their work, and this probably is the work of one guy. Add to that the black bag she was carrying was from Barney a clothing store in New York. If he's still in the business, I'll find him."

Commander Cohen folded his arms and stared at me. "You've been pretty quiet, Jake. What makes you think the white shirts upstairs are going to let me spend a few thousand dollars of the department's money when the people in New York can do this job."

I backed my partner and looked at Cohen in the eyes.

"Between the Barneys bag and the tattoo, I think Sam's right. New York has to be the key. Besides, the cops there have too much on their plate to spend quality time on some bullshit killing by a Midwest hooker. Sam knows the territory, sir. We can run this lead down and be back in no time," I added "My partner knows what he's doing. If he thinks he can come up with it faster than the people in New York, then let's take a shot."

"You've both been warned. If this trip doesn't turn up with a suspect, the brass upstairs is going to be all over me like stink on shit. And by the way. Make sure you check in with the New York police department. And now, the F.B.I has asked us to provide them with copies of our files on Mr. Thompson."

Chapter 13

Illinois Senator Mike Morrison picked up his throwaway cell and tapped in the number of his contact in New York.

"The first piece of the puzzle is in place," he said with a smile on his face. "The cops in Cincinnati think the killer's a New Yorker."

"How's that, Mike?"

"My man in Cincy just called. It seems that the killer had a Trinacria tattooed on her left calf."

"A what?"

"The Medusa. It's on the flag of Sicily," Morrison said.

"Why New York?"

"That should be obvious to you. You're in the Big Apple. Tell me where else outside of Sicily would you see a tattoo like that?" Morrison asked.

"You think the killer is here, in New York?"

"No, but they think she's from the city, or involved with someone from one of Andronni's family," Morrison replied. "That kind of tattoo is only found on wise guys or their girlfriends."

"Ironic, isn't it? Andronni, is not going to like this. I think he's from Sicily. This is going to make the discussion with him more difficult it could be one of his own. This is not the time to give him any problems. He's got shingles, and my people tell me his back is on fire."

Morrison asked, "Oh, I didn't know that. What does Andronni's doctors say?"

"No cure. He has to ride it out. He told his doctor that if he didn't give him something to get rid of the shit, he'd have him whacked."

"You're kidding. He wasn't serious was he?" Morrison asked.

"I doubt it; his doctor is his brother-in-law."

"How long has he had it?"

"Three months. You know how he is. He's tough to talk to when he's feeling great. More important he likes to think he's the sharp end of a stick. Now he feels like shit, and if he doesn't get his hands on the flash drive, he's going to have all of us looking for her."

"There are two detectives from District 1 in Cincinnati coming your way tonight to find the artist who put that on her," Morrison said.

"The investigation's moved here, to New York?" The voice asked.

"They're going to try and find out who drew the tattoo on her," Morrison said.

"This is a big city. It's not going to be easy finding whoever did that work."

"That's where our New York connection comes in. He's got the kind of people that can run this lead down," Morrison reminded him.

"Do you want him to have his men do the cops?"

"For Christ's sake, no. Just get to the tattoo artist before they do, and find out who she is. I think his people should start with the parlors in lower Manhattan."

"You're right, Mike," the voice displayed a sound of excitement. "Our friend the landlord or runs most of the small businesses in Little Italy."

"Exactly. Make sure he tells his people they're not to kill her until we get a good look at what she took," Morrison urged.

"You know he's a sadistic bastard. He doesn't take prisoners. He's going to enjoy making her disappear."

"We want to see what she has first. Once that happens Andronni can do anything he wants with her", Morrison said.

*   *   *

Senator Morrison's contact in New York hung up his phone. He knew the senator was right, and the next call would not be pleasant. He had to keep Joey Andronni's voice down to a dull roar so he could give the mob boss the kind of information that would put a smile on his face. Joey having the shingles wasn't going to make his task easier.

Lisa

Chapter 14

"You screwed up my credit, Carmine. I tried to buy lunch for my friend, Crystal, and they pulled my Visa card. I invite her to lunch, and for Christ's sake, she had to pick up the tab."

"Who the fuck do you think you're talking to," Carmine said, slapping me to the floor. "I get you a job in Dave's club, see to it that you have a roof over your head, and you give me some shit about using some of your money to take care of you?"

"Take care of me?" I answered. "You guinea bastard, you're using my money to pay off your gambling debts."

"My debts?" he said, reaching down, and slapping me again. "If you don't like it around here, get out in the real world, and see what it's like trying to live on your own."

Thanks to Carmine, my Visa, MasterCard, and American Express cards were all canceled. Deep in gambling debt, he used my credit cards to get even with his bookies and put my credit rating in the toilet. My accounts were drained because I was dumb enough to give Carmine my ATM passwords. His words are still poking around in my head.

"I need your password if you expect me to buy our dinner, take you out on the town, or buy you something for your birthday."

At the same time, he always managed to take some out for

himself. Since I worked, and the lazy bastard didn't, he intercepted the mail. He spent the maximum and paid the minimum.

* * *

Thanks to Carmine, I got screwed without getting kissed. The only positive thing I could take from my relationship with the little shit was that he taught me how to use a gun. That led me to be a hitter. But that's another story.

I'm a pretty good shot. Guns, the noise, and their kick never bothered me. Carmine would take me to another connected friend's place on Rocky Point, Long Island. We'd spend the afternoon setting up targets and firing his .38 revolver. I was a better shot than he was and that pissed him off.

Carmine didn't see Nick, the Astoria bookie, the week following the Santucci shooting. One of John Gotti's flunkies replaced Nick. Six months later, the Gotti family put out a contract on Carmine. They got even for him muscling in on their territory. Since he wasn't a made man or a Sicilian someone pushed a button on him, and there were no questions asked. I must admit I was glad. I'd been carrying him, and he was getting fucking heavy.

* * *

When I married my husband, Mark Turnbull, after Carmine was whacked, I believed, as most do, it would be for life. Wrong again. Some escorts have the problem of falling for their customers. He was the exact opposite of Carmine. Mark knew what to do in bed, and it wasn't snoring. I didn't realize he was a habitual drunk who was climbing back on the wagon when I met him.

He spent the two years of his life after we were married in The Attica Correctional Facility in upstate New York. Being in the slammer didn't stop him from drinking. The inmates make their own booze called Pruno. It's a prison wine made from fruit, sugar, ketchup, and water. Inmates could piss in it, but it was so vile, to begin with, they'd never notice the difference.

Mark was stabbed to death with the end of a sharpened spoon

during a fight with another prisoner a month before he was to get out of the slammer. So much for lifelong marriage bliss, when he was ushered off to Hell, I was forced to go back to the escort agency. Why do I always hook up with someone who's on the wrong side of the law? Why can't I meet a regular guy and slide into a normal life?

I could have started in the escort business right after high school. All I needed was a guy like Carmine to whisper in my ear about how much money I could make. It was his friend Dave who got me started selling my body and introduced me to coke.

The day after the state put Mark in the ground Dave got me a job as a high-class party girl. The Agency serviced the Atlantic City casinos. The money was good, but the men using the service were pathetic.

Dave got me all the 'nose candy' I wanted. When he couldn't get me what I needed, I partied with johns who provided me with a pack.

I'm not proud of how I've led my life since I dropped out of high school and surrounded myself with lowlifes, what the hell did I expect?

Most tricks treat escorts like animals. Men who pay for sex think they own the escort who's servicing them. My first rough encounter was at The Boardwalk Casino with a man in his sixties. He wanted an all-nighter. I thought an all-nighter for a man his age meant not getting up to pee.

I started to take my clothes off.

"Keep your clothes on, get on your knees, and bend over. I want to do it with your clothes on."

"With my clothes? Why?"

"I want to make it seem like I'm raping you."

Men, they're all pathetic. Whether you're with them for an hour, a week, or a year, they're only good for one thing. Come to think of it, most of them aren't even good at that.

Jake

Chapter 15

I had hoped everything would fall into place for Veronica and me, so I called her and asked her to meet me for a few drinks at one of the local eateries, The Cock N Bull. It's on the Kentucky side of the river and less than fifteen minutes from the airport. I figured that it would give us more time to be together.

I showered, shaved, and dressed in a knitted pullover I bought at Dillard's yesterday. I looked again in the mirror, brushed back my blonde hair, and headed for the door.

I pulled in front of the restaurant just as Veronica arrived. She stepped out of her car, using a move that showed off her long tanned slender legs. With that body, she makes most women look like boys.

I should miss the flight and meet Sam in the morning.

She looked at the old red brick building. "Hi, Jake," Veronica said, "I've never been here before."

"It's an English-style pub. Great selection of beer."

"Do we have enough time for a drink or two before you have to catch your plane?" She said looping her arm around mine.

I looked at my watch. It was a little before seven. "Yeah, I think so. I'm meeting Sam at the airport at around 8:30."

Veronica said, "This looks like a nice place to have a few drinks and dinner."

"Believe me, if we were having dinner together, it wouldn't be here."

"Oh," she asked with a seductive smile, "where then?"

"Someplace with soft candlelight where I would order us two medium-rare center-cut filet mignons and a bottle of a Napa Valley Cabernet Sauvignon."

She reached out her hand. "Save that for when you get back. It's warm. Let's get a table outside."

After we were seated, we were given menus and ordered our drinks. When the waitress left Veronica asked, "How on earth did you talk Cohen into letting you go to New York to find a tattoo artist?"

"Sam told Cohen that he had worked on a case where a perp had a tattoo like the one that's on our killer's leg. The killer was carrying a shopping bag from a New York clothing store. Put those two together, and Cohen said yes."

"That's one hell of a break," she said.

I laughed. "No, the tattoo business was just Sam's way of talking Cohen into getting his way. I doubt if he knows the artist who did this work. He does that sometimes. Sam has some imagination."

"It won't be fun if you don't come back with a name," Veronica said. "Suppose the tattoo wasn't done in New York? This could be a wild goose chase."

"I know," I shrugged, "but Sam's got a feel for this sort of thing."

"Better than New York's finest?"

"He still thinks he's one of New York's finest."

This was the first time Veronica, and I was alone together away from the job. I wanted to get off the subject of our investigation and on to investigating Veronica close up.

The waitress returned with our drinks. I handed her the menus.

"We're not eating. Just keep us in drinks, please."

Veronica's blue eyes met mine. She gave me a warm smile and took a sip of her wine.

I glanced at my watch. Veronica noticed and said, "What time is your flight?"

I drained my St. Peter's Cream Stout and smiled at her, "9:45. I have to go, even though I'd rather be here with you. I'm sure Sam is pacing the Delta terminal waiting to brag about how he tamed crime in the Naked City."

Veronica said. "It's about a fifteen-minute drive to the airport. If I drive, you won't have to park. We'll have enough time to enjoy another drink."

"What do I do with my car?"

Her voice dropped to a whisper. "You're a cop. Tell the manager you're going to leave it parked on the street, in front of the restaurant, for a few days."

"Okay," I said, "but if you drive you won't be able to get me out of your car."

"There'll be time for us when you get back. How long do you think you guys are going to be gone?"

"Long enough to make me hurry back for a night with you at the Grand Finale," I replied. "If Sam is as good as he says he is we should be back in a couple of days."

I didn't want to talk shop to this lovely lady. It looked like a good time to change the subject. "We've worked together for the last two years, and I know very little about you."

"Where should I start?" she asked.

"Start at the beginning. Where're you from?"

"Well, I'm from Dayton, and moved to Cincinnati when my dad was transferred here."

"That's the first thing we have in common. I was born in Cincinnati. I got my law degree at the University of Dayton."

"I didn't know you're a lawyer."

"Yes, but I've never really hung a shingle."

"Forgive me if it sounds like I'm prying, but I understand you were married."

"Yeah, the usual story. We were too young. We met at UD, and when I graduated, we got married. But that's enough about me. How come you're still on the loose?"

"I haven't found the right guy who doesn't mind the work I do."

"Tough job, cutting up the dead, isn't it?"

"A pathology degree isn't for the faint of heart."

"This is one of the few times we've seen each other outside the lab."

"That's because lab work is considered a large part of my job and where I spend most of my time."

"I hadn't realized how much work went into being an M.E."
She smiled and took my hand. "That's enough about me. Tell me more about you."

"Not now. I plan for you to get to know me better when we're alone."

She picked up her wine and sipped. A light breeze floated through her hair as she smiled at me. I drew a breath and looked into her eyes. I reached over and took her hand in mine. I leaned closer to her and pressed my lips to hers. The kiss was soft. I let it linger, hoping she wouldn't pull away; she didn't.

"We can continue getting to know each other when I get back," I said.

She blushed and slowly pulled away. Her bright eyes looked at mine.

"Let's toast your trip to New York, and hope you find the artist who worked on our killer. We don't have to go out. I can cook us dinner at my place."

"No, the Grand Finale, Miratage, it doesn't matter. I'll be there before they open."

I kissed her softly on the lips, and we went to her car.

Chapter 16

New York City, New York

Joey "The Priest" Andronni was born in western Sicily in 1949. He was the son of illiterate peasants from Bagheria. His parents roamed the hills outside of Palermo tending sheep. As a youth, Joey wanted no part of being a sheepherder.

Most Sicilians are short and olive-skinned. Joe was no exception. His build was stocky but muscular. Touches of gray-streaked his thinning wavy hair. His dark eyes sat in the shadows under large bushy eyebrows with startling manic energy. When he spoke his voice sounded as if he had swallowed a bag of gravel. Andronni had the look of a farmer; in truth, he was a was a killer.

In the early sixties, when Joey was thirteen years old, his parents immigrated to the United States. At their insistence, he went to the seminary after he graduated high school. He spent two years at the school but abandoned the calling when it became clear to him that he'd be expected to work for his flock, not the other way around.

Living in the Bay Ridge, the 'little Italy' section of Brooklyn, Andronni was surrounded by 'the wise guys.' He started in the rackets as a bouncer in a brothel run by Carlo DeBruzzi, a captain of the Joe Colombo family. Joey became the family's problem solver and eventually rose to second in command.

When Al 'The Ox' Cataldi ratted Carlo out, Carlo went to prison for drug trafficking. That's when Andronni seized control of the family from the remnants of the Colombo regime. He was soon the reigning mafia boss in New York City.

Other members of New York's crime scene knew Joey as somewhat of an oddball. He called people he didn't have respect for, 'friend.'

When he was a young hitter, because of his training in the seminary, he often gave his victims their last rites as they lay dying. He said he was cleansing their soul for their voyage to meet the Lord.

Apart from his prostitution and heroin businesses, which were looked down on by the other New York Dons, he had an iron-fisted control of the waterfront unions and their pension funds.

By the late-nineties Andronni had become, behind the scenes, a major player in New York's political landscape. He eventually became a benefactor to a senator from Illinois and the three borough presidents in New York City.

*   *   *

Looking out his office window at Lake Michigan, Senator Morrison said, "Are you using the phone a gave you, Joey?"

"Of course. I'm using one of those throwaway phones you sent me. You know how I hate talking on the phone."

Morrison said, "My people in Ohio tell me the murder investigation of Hank has moved to New York."

Andronni asked quickly. "Why here?"

"Something about a Sicilian tattoo. By the way," Morrison continued, "that was a piece of genius using a woman to do away with Hank."

Andronni's voice went down in volume, and up in intensity. "A woman? I hate to burst your bubble, senator, but I didn't have him whacked."

"This is no time to be funny, Joey. The deal was to get to Hank before the F.B.I. did." Morrison paused and raised his voice. "Are you telling me she didn't send you the information from his computer?"

"Didn't you hear me, friend? I didn't do the bastard. I thought you did. And don't raise your fucking voice like that to me again. What's with all this bullshit about his computer anyway? I thought you were getting rid of him, so he couldn't testify about the scheme you used with my union funds to run your campaign."

"Whoever killed him drained his computer. Hank might have had information about some of our operations on his laptop. The Justice Department was one step behind the bastard ready to indict him."

"It's a good thing I'm not driving a fucking car, my friend. You're putting me to sleep. What's this *our* shit?"

"You're involved, too," Morrison said. "That's not the whole problem, Joey. It goes deeper than that, and frankly, I don't have the time to explain."

"Look, senator, your attitude is beginning to bother me more than these fucking shingles I have on my back."

"I'm sorry you're not feeling well, Joey, but he may have all the figures on our Thailand operation, and you're controlling the union funds."

"That's your problem, friend, not mine. The drug shit is yours. I only give a damn about the other businesses."

"But this could be your problem, too," Morrison said, as gently as he could. "If the drug operation is on the flash drive, then your name could be on it, too."

"My name? Who the fuck uses names? If my name was on that computer," he paused, "you'll follow your friend, Hank." Andronni raised his voice. "Hank was your guy, not mine. You put him in place and said he was safe. Now I find that the idiot may have put my shit on his computer. Don't screw with me. I could have you in the ground before you make your next horseshit speech. You're in Washington because I put you there. You didn't get elected because you're charming or had some great plan for the people in Illinois. The only thing you did for Chicago is bought a house, and that deal was shady. Like Kennedy, you got elected because my people bought you a state."

"That's not funny," Morrison said. "You're talking to the United

States Senator."

"Is that supposed to make me shit my pants?"

"Look, we've got a man on the Cincinnati police force looking after our interests," Morrison said. "I've got my people looking for her. Chances are there's nothing on it."

"Listen to me, my friend. 'Chances Are' is a song I listened to when I was in the back seat of my car fucking your girlfriend. In my business, Senator Morrison, it's not healthy for me to take chances or trust anyone."

* * *

Andronni threw the phone down. He pulled himself out of his chair and ground his cigar in the ashtray. "This guy can't be trusted," he muttered. He pressed the button mounted under his desk that summoned his bodyguard.

Within seconds a man appeared and closed the door behind him.

Andronni took out a cigar, bit off one end, and spit it out.

"Get with our people in Washington," Andronni said, "and have them keep an eye on our senator friend. I want to know everything this fucking con man does before he does it."

* * *

Morrison was shaking. He reached into a drawer in his desk and pulled out a bottle and poured a large glass of *Makers Mark*.

With his eyes clenched shut, he muttered, "I hope those shingles burn him to a crisp. The guy is crazy. I'd have the grease ball thrown in the lake, but he'd cause a giant oil spill, and that would get the EPA all over my ass."

Jake

Chapter 17

Delta Flight 1756 lifted off at 8:55 pm, whisking Sam and myself to New York. My partner has a gift for gab. I made the mistake of telling Sam this was my first trip to New York. I joking told him I was expecting someone to be rude or try to mug me. I almost fell asleep listening to him drone on about the histories of the Empire State Building, the Statue of Liberty, the subway system and Times Square. I tried to give him the history of the Tyler Davidson Fountain, in downtown Cincinnati, and how it was designed to rival the fountains of Europe, but he did   what I should have done; he fell asleep.

The good news was that we weren't going to share a hotel room. The bad news, Sam's partner, Christopher, decided to come along and might get in the way of the investigation, but he was on a buying trip, and Sam was excited about visiting their old hangouts together. I guess Christopher didn't want Sam to be alone in the Big Apple.

When we landed at La Guardia, my partner acted like a kid whose father bought him a new computer game. He ran through the terminal giving people the high-five and screaming, "I love New York." I had to jog to keep up with him.

"Slow up," I yelled. "Times Square never closes, remember?"

"That's Vegas. Traffic into the city is going to be a bitch this time of the evening."

"What the hell are you talking? I asked. "It's almost midnight."

On the way to the baggage area, Sam brought me up to speed on how he thought we should conduct our search for the artist who drew the tattoo.

"We'll start in Soho. If that doesn't produce any results, we'll check out Chinatown. There are a couple of places on Canal Street that do this kind of work."

I shook my head at him and faked a smile. "Soho? I thought you said we weren't sharing the same room."

"Not in the same room, Tracy, in the same hotel. Since Chris is on a buying trip, the store is paying for his room. It's cheap, and Commander Cohen okayed the place. Our hotel is right in the same neighborhood where most of the tattoo artists do business."

"Let's start where your robbery investigation ended."

"What investigation?"

"The story you told Cohen."

"You didn't believe that bullshit, did you? That was just a story to get us here. You know me better than that."

"I thought so. I wanted to hear it from you."

"As I said before, we'll start in Soho."

"What about Little Italy?" I asked. "Didn't you say the Trinacria was a Sicilian figure?"

"Yeah, but I called a few friends at my old precinct. Joey Andronni, the boss who runs all of Manhattan, kicked the tattoo parlors into Chinatown and Soho."

"Why'd he do that?"

"Something about only lowlifes have tattoos. If he doesn't own most of the stores and businesses in Little Italy, he controls them."

My partner took charge when we exited the terminal. He jumped in front of a cab, flashed his badge, which caused the cab to come to a screeching halt. He yanked open the back door and pushed me in.

"WHAT THE HELL ARE YOU DOING?" the driver screamed.

"A cab driver speaking English, now there's a surprise," Sam said. "I'm commandeering this vehicle. Get us to the Lyceum

Hotel. It's on the corner of Sixth Avenue and Broadway."

The driver interrupted, turned, and looked at Sam. Let me see some more I.D."

"Here it is again," my partner said, sticking his gold badge in the driver's face.

"You want me to take the bridge or the tunnel?"

He turned back and shifted his eyes to the rearview mirror.

"Don't use the Fifty-Ninth Street Bridge. Use the tunnel. I'm a cop, remember." Sam reminded the driver. "Hurry. We're on police business."

"You're telling a stranger we're on police business?"

"That's how you get things done in the big city," Sam said. "Oh, and by the way, I forgot to mention I'm meeting a few old friends at a bar in the village. Naturally, you're coming."

"You want to take me to a gay bar?"

"Now that you've got a woodie for Veronica, you don't want to drink with me?"

"For crying out loud, what the hell am I going to do in a gay bar?"

"Why don't you come and find out?"

"No."

"Come on; you might like my friends," Sam said, patting me on the thigh and squeezing it. "It'll be fun seeing how the other half lives."

I shot back, "The other half? That's a joke."

Sam tapped his badge against the plastic barrier. "Hey, man, open this damn thing up."

He looked back in the mirror at Sam. "I can't. I gotta keep it closed for my safety."

"We're cops," Sam reminded him.

"Do you think I'm an idiot? You could have bought that badge on Times Square. I've got a mind to take you to the nearest police station."

Good idea. We need to check in with the local police anyway.

"If you're going to take us in, make it the Sixth Precinct. It's on Tenth Street between Bleecker and Hudson."

"I know where it is."

"Why the Sixth?" I asked.

"That's my old precinct. It's up the street from The Brickyard Tavern. That's the bar we're going to later. It's the best after-hours gay club in Manhattan."

The driver looked again in the mirror, shook his head, turned right, and smiled.

I hope he doesn't think I'm gay.

The cab ducked into the Queens-Midtown Tunnel. Five minutes later we exited at Thirty-Seventh Street and swung south along Second Avenue.

On the drive, I sat back and laid out the rules for this trip.

"We're not here to hopscotch gay bars so you can catch up with your friends. We're here to find the connection between the artist and the killer, period."

"Lighten up, Jake. I know why we're here. We can mix business with a little pleasure."

I reminded him. "Very little,"

Sam was right, the traffic along the East River at this hour was heavy, but it took only twenty minutes for the ride from the tunnel exit to the Sixth Precinct. The driver snapped the meter lever down and pushed the moneybox through the opening in the plastic barrier. His eyes met mine in the mirror. "$35.65 for the ride, six-fifty for the tunnel, that's $42.15."

Sam jammed his hand in his pocket and pulled out a roll of bills.

"Give me a ten, will ya, Jake?" I've only got twenties here."

"You're a big tipper. Give the driver sixty. The guy speaks English."

We took our bags from the cab, dodging the uniformed police that passed in and out through the huge wooden front doors. Blue and white cruisers blocked half the street in front of the building.

Sam said, "I worked here when I got out of the academy." He slung his bag over his shoulder and motioned me inside.

Our station house in Cincinnati had the same dank smell. The scene at the front desk looked like someone had unloaded an ark full of perps.

The men dressed in Armani suits were mixed in with skanky

looking hookers, their pimps, and whatever was roaming the streets tonight.

My eyes bounced back and forth between the detectives, the cops, and their charges. The place boiled with action. I pushed my way through a crowd of uniforms, shoving cuffed suspects along the corridors. The hookers were trying to talk their way back onto the streets telling the cops they needed to earn. Instantly I felt at home. But unlike our district in Cincinnati, the trail of cops and cuffed bodies seemed to have no end.

The crusty old potbellied sergeant manning the front desk was giving orders to anyone who would listen. Pointing to a wire basket, he shouted, "Preliminary paperwork in the basket, perps in the back. And don't forget to hand in the finished reports."

"Hey, DePasquale," Sam greeted the desk sergeant. "You're still pushing paper?"

The sergeant's head jerked up, and in a deep voice he rumbled, "My God, is that you Sam?" He pushed aside a mound of paper and came around the desk and grabbed Sam in a bear hug.

"Don't tell me you're back on the job as the detective assigned here?"

Sam said, "No, my partner and I are running down a lead on a Cincy murder."

The sergeant's eyebrows went up, and I caught him staring at me.

His partner? My God, I hope he doesn't think I'm….

"We think the killer is from here or at least spent some time in New York," Sam said.

"Why?" the sergeant asked.

"There's a Trinacria on the killer's leg."

His brown eyes bulged. "Lots of luck." He pointed over his shoulder.

"The Medusa? Half of the guys in those cell blocks, back there, have that tattoo."

I looked at my watch and was surprised to see it was after midnight. My day had started at 7:30 a.m. in Ohio. I had a few drinks in Kentucky, trying to score with a beautiful woman, and now I'm here in New York getting ready to drink in a gay bar.

I grabbed Sam by the arm, pulled him across the room, and said, "If there're guys in the back with this type of tattoo, let's start asking them where they got it. I don't think we'll get that information in a gay nightclub."

* * *

The Brickyard Tavern was high-ceilinged old stucco-styled New York sports pub converted into a gay nightclub. In front of the building stood a small desk flanked by two large men dressed in tuxedos. They smiled, waved us toward the entrance, and reached under the counter for an umbrella. Lightning flashed across the sky. It began to rain.

I popped a few aspirins and wished Sam had given me a heads up on what to expect.

I've been in gay bars before, but it was to break up a fight or collar a perp.

The second I walked through the door I should have taken a U-turn. This was not a sports bar. At least, not the kind of gay sports bars you find on the north side of Cincinnati. A bar filled with men dancing and kissing was not my usual hangout.

Over the archway entrance was a sign that read:

'Uncontrollable Excitement Awaits Those
Who Pass
Through This Cosmic Rainbow.'

The wallpaper gave the illusion of marijuana plants growing up pale yellow walls. The place had high ceilings, and strobe lights, where everyone danced to loud disco music. Marble floors polished to a high sheen brought to mind pictures I had seen of the famous Studio 54. The second floor, Sam said, had several private lounges. A sign hung over the mahogany bar read,

'Wrap your lips around the bartender or a
delicious martini.'

At the far end of the room were two dark, empty stages. I tried to raise my voice above the music. "I can hardly hear myself think, Sam. There are a lot of young guys here. I'm in my fifties, and bit long in the tooth to be drinking with kids."

"It's okay. Guys older than you hang out here. No one will bother you. Stay close to me and enjoy the view."

Suddenly the loud beat changed and the noise died down. Guys were swaying to the soft music while they massaged each other's crotches.

Sam grabbed me by the arm and twisted me toward the bar.

"Don't stare at the flaming bitches. They love being watched and play off the attention."

"What's a flaming bitch?"

"You don't wanna know."

"Tell me anyway."

"They're the ones who are outrageously dressed. They put on the best show, but they're harmless. It's the bottom boys, the scrubwomen dressed in heavy leather. Order yourself a beer and stay away from the men's room."

"Scrub-woman? What the hell is that?"

Sam shook his head. "That's another thing you don't want to know. I'm sorry, Jake. I keep forgetting how clueless you are." He pointed to the two guys seated at a table next to the men's room. "They're scrub-women. They have to have sex all the time. Don't go near them."

"What if I have to take a leak?"

"If you go into the toilet, they'll think you're looking to hook-up, and I mean literally hook-up. Hold it, or look for me, and I'll take you in."

"But what if I still get hit on?"

"Don't worry. I'll take care of you. I can bitch slap with the best of them."

"I didn't know you were that tough with bitches," I said, laughing.

"Tough? Imagine how tough I'd be if I weren't Catholic."

"Catholic? I've never heard of you going to confession."

"I do it online. And," he said, pointing to a dark-skinned guy at the end of the bar, "stay away from that dairy queen."

"Dairy Queen, what the hell?" I looked away. "Don't tell me. I don't want to know. One beer and I'm out of here. They do serve beer here, don't they?"

"Of course they do," he said. "This is *not* the normal gay scene. You only find nightclubs like this in Frisco, Chicago, Philly, Miami and L.A. Most gay bars or clubs are just like straight bars, no flaming boys. Some have dance floors, and some even have gay women."

Sam put his hand on my back, pushing me toward the bar.

"This is a fun place. Just enjoy it. Oh, and get us two seats up front," he added pointing to the stage. "The show will start around midnight."

"What show?"

"They have a midnight performer here. The feature act makes a grand entrance, flutters through the crowd blowing kisses, and then puts on a show."

Sam wove through the crowd kissing his friends hello, and patting strangers on the ass. This was a side of my partner I'd never seen. Being in New York meant he was back in his element. In Cincinnati, he kept his lifestyle under wraps.

At the bar, I sat next to a couple of guys that looked like they belonged on the cover of GQ.

One of the GQs asked, "How they hanging?"

"Fine," I said looking back over my shoulder, "and how are yours hanging?" I answered trying to act laid-back. How are yours hanging? Now, why the hell did I say that? I still think Dairy Queen is a place you buy ice cream.

He laughed, shook his head. "Two in a bunch, one for breakfast, one for lunch, and you know what I like for dinner."

That got me off the bar stool heading straight for the front door, but he followed me. He patted my butt and squeezed it. I grabbed his wrist twisting it. I didn't have to exert much pressure. He went down like a feather.

A crooked smile spread across his face. "You want me here, sweetie?" he said.

I reached into my pocket, yanked out my badge, and jammed it up his nose. Sam was standing behind the guy, doubled over with laughter.

The strange thing is, we were in a room full of people, and no one stopped to look at the action I had tangled myself in.

Sam cried out, "Welcome to my world."

"Now there's an ugly thought, Catchem."

This bar wasn't the place for me. I went over to the window and saw the two tuxedoed valets standing underneath a large umbrella. Suddenly a white Bentley drove up to the front of the club and screeched to a halt. One of the parking attendants stepped out from under the umbrella, opened the passenger door, and extended his hand. A flamboyant guy in a white jacket, without a shirt, and with a black scarf wrapped around his neck stepped out of the car, grabbed the valet's hand, and kissed it. He moved like silk in the wind. The dancer, with big eyes, peered through large heart-shaped glasses perched on his nose. The other tuxedoed valet opened the club door. The guy pirouetted by me and blew me a kiss.

I stepped out into the rain with the sound of applause screaming in my ears.

I found New York to be everything it was stacked up to be, but not for me. I had to find my comfort zone. Where the hell is the Sixth Precinct?

Jake

Chapter 18

I left the club intending to revisit the Sixth Precinct and question the perps who had the Trinacria tattoos. The rain came down in sheets, but there were plenty of storefront awnings to walk under to keep me dry. Even though most of the stores along the street were closed, their windows were well lit.

You don't see many panhandlers in Cincinnati, at least not many after midnight, Certainly, none working in the rain. But since this was my first time in New York, nothing surprised me. It was just my luck a bum was set up in the doorway of a closed store, licking his chops, waiting for me to walk by. I must have looked like a pig on a spit with a shiny red apple in its mouth. He sat with his back against the entrance of the store frowning as I approached. His hair hung down to his shoulders. A scraggly gray beard and pointy nose accented his face. The guy was wearing a quilted vest, matted with dirt, over a short sleeve shirt. He could have been one of the guys who put the deal together for the purchase of Manhattan from the Indians or rowed the boat for George Washington when he crossed the Delaware. Well, maybe he wasn't that old, but you could see veins peeking through his thin skin. His left eye had a tic.

"Help a Viet Nam vet get out of da rain and get a decent meal," he said, holding out a cigar box with a few dollar bills in it.

"I'm out of change," I said, trying to drift by.

He got to his feet and slapped one hand to his side. "I can take bills. Change won't get you much of a a meal in the Big Apple."

I didn't want to get wet, but having the rain coming down like bullets on my head was a damn sight better than having to deal with this bum; so I stepped out from under the awning. I know in some religions giving alms to the poor may earn you points in the hereafter, but I'm in the here. I'll let the hereafter take care of itself.

"Sorry, I'm in a rush."

He looked past me as a blue-and-white police cruiser pulled up to the curb.

He said, "Never mind. Gotta go." He closed the box and stashed it under his arm.

And that's when I saw a tattoo on the underside of his forearm. It was a smaller version of the one on our killer's leg, but clearly a Trinacria.

I grabbed his bony arm and twisted it to get a better look. He flashed me a disgruntled look and pulled away. "Hey, get your hands off me! What the hell are you doing?"

"Where'd you get this?" I took my badge from my pocket and shoved it in his face. "I'm a cop."

"Look, leave me alone, will ya?"

"I'm a cop. That's what I do. Ask questions."

"And I'm a beggar, that's what I do, beg. Besides, ya can't be a cop. I know all the frickin' cops on this beat. Where'd you get that badge, on line?"

"I'm from Cincinnati."

"That's great. Mayor Bloomberg is farming out cops."

I pointed to his arm. "Where'd you get that?"

"I was born with the fricking thing and I gotta nudda one on the udder side."

"I mean the tattoo."

The guy squirmed from my grasp. "I don't remember."

The cruiser door opened and a uniformed cop emerged decked out in a navy blue uniform. He was dressed in navy from head to toe in the same color. Even his hat was the same color.

"What's the problem here, sir?" he asked. "Is this guy bothering ya?"

Since my badge was in the bum's face, I showed it to the cop.

"I'm a Cincinnati detective following up a lead, and I need to take this clown in for questioning."

"Let me see some more ID."

I yanked out my Fraternal Order of Police membership card, a precinct ID with my picture on it, and my driver's license.

"Have you checked in with our people?"

"Yeah, my partner and I, Sam Ferris, checked in earlier up the street with a Sergeant DePasquale."

He cocked his head and smiled at me. "I know Sam. He's your partner?"

Oh no, there's that look again.

I said, "Yeah, he's my street partner."

The cop laughed. "I see you've got your evening wear on, Shudda."

"Evening wear?" I asked.

"Shudda cleans up during the day so he can look good working the crowd at the racetrack."

Shudda pleaded. "I'm getting wet. Can we get outta the rain?"

"Yeah, sure. Shudda," the cop said, pointing his nightstick at him. "Stay put. Officer O'Brien is in the cruiser, and you know how he likes chasing you."

"Yeah, last week he chased me into a moving cab. I Shudda sued his ass."

The officer doubled over laughing. "You want to take Shudda in? We don't take him off the street. We chase him off the street. He's harmless."

"I need to ask him some questions about this tattoo he has on his arm."

Shudda looked at me as though I had fallen out of the sky.

"You wanna ask me about my tattoo? Don't they have tattoos in Bumblefuck, Ohio?"

"Cincinnati," I reminded him.

"Whatever."

"Come on, Shudda, get in the car," the officer pushed him toward the cruiser. "By the way, Shudda, who do you like in the feature at Belmont tomorrow."

*   *   *

When we got to the station, the desk sergeant I had met earlier was still on duty. The stale odor and smoke inside still lingered. Seeing just the two of us, he nodded and poured coffee into a cup with a New York Yankees logo on it.

Sergeant DePasquale turned his head to look at the wall clock behind him. "Sam still at The Brickyard? I guess the midnight show at the club has already started. You're missing all the fun."

"Yes," I said. "I felt like General Custer at the Little Big Horn."

"Don't you guys have a club like that in Cleveland?" DePasquale asked.

"Cincinnati, damn it," I said, rolling my eyes.

"No, we don't."

"I see you got Shudda with you. What are you doing here, Shudda?"

"I brought him in for questioning."

"Shudda? Questioning? He's not touting you, is he?"

I wonder if touting is another gay expression. I pulled out the police photo of the killer's tattoo.

"He's got a tattoo like this one here."

The sergeant asked, pointing to the photo.

"Does that look familiar, Shudda?"

Shudda said, "Could be 'Harry the Horse, Eddie 'the Mark', or 'Vinnie DeMilo's' work. Eddie did mine."

"Why did you have a Sicilian symbol put on your arm?" I asked Shudda.

"Cause I'm Sicilian, dipshit."

"And who's Harry the Horse?" I asked.

The sergeant took a sip of his coffee. "He's a tattoo artist over on Canal Street."

"Shudda, Harry the Horse, Vinnie DeMilo, where did you guys get these names?"

"Harry's called the horse cause he's got horses' heads tattooed all over his back and a silver one on his chest."

"And Vinnie DeMilo?"

DePasquale said. "That could be his, but it doesn't matter. He's room temperature,"

"And Shudda here?" I asked, shooting a glance at Shudda. "What kind of a name is Shudda?"

"Shudda's a tout. You do have a racetrack in Cleveland, don't you?" asked the sergeant.

"Cincinnati, for Christ's sake," I reminded him. "Yeah, we've got racetracks. Beltera Park in Cincinnati and Turfway Park over in Kentucky. And I'm sure you've heard of Churchill Downs."

"Shudda's real name is Salvatore. Right, Shudda?"

The dirt bag nodded.

"He's a green sheeter," the sergeant repeated.

I didn't parachute in here yesterday, but after twenty years on the force, the word didn't ring a bell. "What's a green sheeter?" I asked.

"He's the guy at the race track who give you green and yellow sheets with information on what horses to bet, for a donation of course."

"He gives you winners?" I asked.

The sergeant laughed. "That's a joke. Does the guy standing next to you look like he's a winner?"

Shudda's eyes almost bulged out of his head as he gave the sergeant a dirty look. He looked at me as if he'd just been insulted.

"When the horse he tells you to bet on loses, he always has an excuse for why it lost." He paused and looked at Shudda. "Always an excuse, huh, Shudda. The jockey shudda gone to the front, the track shudda been fast, you shudda played him to finish third. The jockey let the horse get boxed in. The race was fixed. Get the picture?" he asked. "Shudda this, shudda that, most of the guys here think you're full of shitta, Shudda."

"Speaking of pictures," Shudda took the photo out of my hands. "Can I get another look at this?"

"Here," I said. "Be my guest."

"Three guys would do this kind of work. I think this one was done at The Rose Tattoo," he said.

"Rose Tattoo?"

"The Rose Tattoo is Eddie Mark's joint over on Canal Street. Dis looks like his work. He likes to do lotta colors."

I thought for a second. "Eddie's called the mark because he marks up people, right?"

Shudda looked at the sergeant and smiled. "Hey, the rent-a-cop's catching on."

This guy was pissing me off. "Careful, you wise-ass, or you'll wind up in a glue factory with the horses you bet on."

Shudda asked DePasquale, "Isn't Eddie's one of the places Andronni kicked out of Little Italy and into Chinatown?"

"Yeah, he thinks only lowlifes go to tattoo parlors."

"Everyone's got a tattoo nowadays," Shudda looked around and said. "I bet even Joey's girlfriend has one on her fat ass."

I looked up at the ceiling, expecting the name Andronni to jog my memory, but it didn't. "That name doesn't ring a bell. Who's Andronni?" I asked.

DePasquale said, "He's the thug who runs Manhattan."

"You mean he's connected," Shudda said.

"No, he's the connector. All the wise guys in New York are connected to Joey the Priest," DePasquale answered.

"I thought you said Andronni? Who's Joey the Priest?"

"Andronni. He was in the seminary before he became a thug, so they call him 'Joey the Priest.' He quit the church because he figured it was better to receive than to give."

The station started to become active again. Hookers, street kids with their pants hanging under their Asses, and drunks needing a place to sleep, were paraded in front of Sergeant DePasquale.

"It looked like the three o'clock crowd is coming in early. Take Shudda in the back and get what you need from him. Then turn him loose."

As we walked away, Shudda looked over his shoulder. "Hey, Sarge, I got a real hot one in the sixth at Belmont tomorrow."

Lisa

Chapter 19

The phone call from Eddie came out of the blue. "What the hell are you talking about?" I said, barking into my cell, and laying down the morning newspaper.

I hadn't expected to hear from Eddie so soon. We talk and see each other from time to time. In fact, he called a week ago. He was going to close the shop for a few days, and we were going to meet at Atlantic City next week.

"Two of Joey Andronni's crew just left here, Lisa. And those guys were scary looking. Both of them were big enough to walk through a brick wall. They wanted to know if I was the artist who decorated your leg. They were looking for you, and I don't think they were looking to get laid."

I knew they didn't want me. It was the flash drive they were after. After I put Hank to sleep, I was supposed to turn it over to Andronni.

I looked down at my tattoo and ran my hand over it. "You're kidding, my leg? What do they want with me?"

"I have no idea," Eddie said, "but they had a photo of your leg with my drawing on it."

"Where did they get a picture of my leg?"

"They didn't say, but what I'm trying to figure out is why they want you."

My head was swimming, my pulse pounding. "What'd you tell them?"

"It wasn't my work. It looked like Vinnie DeMilo's shit."

"Eddie, DeMilo's been in the ground for five years."

"Yeah, that's the point. Eddie's dead. His old shop is a Chinese takeout. I figured if I told them Vinnie did it, and they know he's in the ground, they'd stop looking."

"And they bought it?"

"Yeah. I think so. These guys look so dumb they probably think a stud finder is a broad looking for a guy."

"I know some of Joey's people. I ran around with Carmine, remember?"

"What's Joey got to do with this?"

"I don't know I haven't done anything to him."

Eddie said, raising his voice. "What's wrong with you, Lisa? You don't know why they want you?" "I know you've gotten soft since you moved to Cincinnati. We're talking about Andronni here. The only people he trusts are the ones who can't breathe. Where is your head?"

Eddie being visited by Andronni's men, and getting my location, could be a problem. Hitters never divulge their whereabouts to a client, and Eddie knows where I live. He could be in big trouble.

I studied the ceiling as though the answer to his next question was going to descend from above.

"I can't imagine why a New York wise guy would be looking for a woman in Cincinnati. What have you done, babe?"

I sucked in my breath, trying to remain calm. I wasn't sure whether I should tell Eddie about the flash drive or the contract I had on Hank.

"Nothing, Eddie. Not a thing."

He wasn't buying it. Eddie raised his voice. "You're not telling me everything, are you?"

I thought for a moment. I had nowhere to turn. I knew I could trust Eddie.

"I hit a guy for Joey."

"Are you crazy? You're still hitting?"

"I gotta make a living. Nobody wants to see a fifty-year-old escort."

"But whoever your go-between is, he's bound to tell Joey who you are."

"He can't now. The guy overdosed a few days after we put the deal together."

"So Joey doesn't know it's you?"

"This lousy tattoo points to me. He doesn't know who I am. But I'm sure that's why his goons are looking all over Manhattan. That's the least of my problems."

"How's that?"

I was supposed to take some info off the mark's computer and send it to Joey."

"Didn't he get it?"

"I didn't send it."

"Why not?"

"When I got home I realized if Joey thinks I saw what's on it, I'm dead."

"And if you didn't look?" Eddie asked.

"I'm dead anyway. As you said, Joey doesn't like women with pulses."

I could hear Eddie breathing hard.

"Well," he continued without coming up for air, "I can't meet on the island next week. "You're in deep shit and now, so am I. Whatever you do don't let a temporary solution turn into a permanent problem."

"I guess you're right," I said, placing my hand on the kitchen table to steady myself. I dropped into a chair. "I can exchange my ticket to Atlantic City for one to Nashville and hide out at my friend Helen's place."

"Nashville? If Joey's looking for you, you wouldn't be safe on the fucking moon."

Not the kind of support I needed to hear. I walked over to the coffee pot and poured myself a cup with shaking hands. I shouldn't have taken this contract.

"I've got a bad feeling about this, babe. These guys are dangerous. Andronni doesn't take prisoners. Don't exchange the ticket. If you're going to Nashville, drive. Pack your car with get-away gear. We'll get together sometime next week. I've got a customer at the door. I gotta go. Bye."

I flipped my cell closed and thought about how I had met Eddie; the night Carmine took me into The Rose Tattoo. I was immediately attracted to him. He was everything Carmine wasn't. Eddie was tall and good-looking, had a great sense of humor, and made an honest living. He played the bass guitar with a rock group.

Carmine, on the other hand, was a piece of shit. His sense of humor revolved around the bookies he strong-armed and they people he cheated.

I wanted a tattoo, and Carmine wanted the Medusa, with snakes coming out of her head, somewhere on my body. Eddie's eyes lit up when I told him I wanted one drawn on each of my boobs with my nipples at its open mouth. I wanted it to be different. But Carmine said 'No way.' It wasn't the money. Carmine was a jealous bastard, and the thought of Eddie touching my chest set him off. We finally decided on the outside of my left calf. He should have put it on the inside.

Months later when Carmine was gunned down, I tried to hook up with Eddie, but he had taken up with some fat broad from Jersey. That's when I met Mark.

When I was touring a few years ago, I ran into Eddie at Belmont Park in New York. One thing led to another, and we spent the weekend together. We've been seeing each other on and off ever since.

I got up, walked across the kitchen, poured myself another cup of coffee, and picked up the *Cincinnati Enquirer*. My cat, Miss Kitty, who thinks she's a guard dog, trotted behind me across the kitchen floor and leaped onto the windowsill.

The headline above the fold stared at me. One of my questions to Eddie was about to be answered.

Have You Seen this Tattoo?
Story on page 4A.

The article was written below a photograph of the Medusa in

living color. I scanned the paper quickly to see if I recognized any of the names in the story, but thank God, except for two detectives on the case, there weren't any.

I shot the guy last week, and it's still news? But it was my leg in the picture. The article stated that the Cincinnati police had released the photo in the hope that someone would recognize the tattoo. The report said the image of the tattoo was taken from a surveillance camera in the hotel. I saw the camera and gave them the finger. Hank wanted me to wear a short dress and heels. I should have worn pants. It now looked like the joke is on me.

I knew this would be trouble. I should have thought that through before I took the contract. Whether I looked at the flash drive or not, I was toast.

When I finished the last sip of the now cold coffee, I walked over to my laptop and set the empty cup down next to it.

Even though I was given some money up front for doing Hank, the cash was running out. I couldn't place another ad in the escort service's website. They're probably looking for me there too. Even though there were always some forty local escorts advertising on the site, there was still a dozen touring. I couldn't take that chance. I'll just call guys I've been with before.

I slid open the top desk drawer. Groping through the paper and pens. I looked for the flash drive that had the numbers of the johns I've partied with in Cincinnati. Instead, I found the one I picked up after the hit. I was curious to see what the big fuss was all about. I placed it in one of the ports of my computer and turned it on. A white page popped up with many files on it.

That's odd. It didn't take me that long to upload the information.

I positioned the arrow over the first icon and clicked it twice. My head shot up. It was a letterhead:

Hank Thompson and Assoc. C.P.A.
711 South Dearborn
Chicago, IL. 60605
312-555-6767

I clicked on the icon that read International Service Workers

Union Funds.

"Oh my God. What have I gotten myself into?"

Jake

Chapter 20

It was after 1 a.m. when I got back to the hotel. Since I'd been on my feet for more than fifteen hours, I got a concussion when my head hit the pillow. Since skyscrapers surrounded this hotel, I'll bet this room has never seen the light of day.

I picked up my cell phone and dialed Sam's room.

After a couple of rings, Chris, his partner, answered.

"Who's this?"

"Jake. Is Sam up?"

"He's just getting out of the shower. Can I have him call you back, sweetie?"

Sweetie? I hope I don't have to spend too much time talking to Sam's partner.

"No, tell him to meet me in the restaurant." I looked over at the clock radio, "at nine."

A few minutes later Sam called me back. He told me he'd meet me in the lobby for coffee.

The Morning After was the Hotel Lyceum's breakfast café. Thirteen dollars for bacon and eggs is obscene. I was still in menu shock when Sam walked up to my table, grabbed me by the arm, pulled me out of my chair, and led me out of the restaurant, and into the lobby.

"Never eat in a New York hotel restaurant."

"You said meet me in the restaurant."

Sam's eyebrows lifted. "No, you said the restaurant. I told you to meet in the lobby. There's coffee there, and it's free."

"I'm hungry, and I haven't had anything since last night."

"But not here in the hotel. There's a coffee shop up the street where you pay seven bucks for scrambled eggs, toast, and all the coffee you can drink. Come on," Sam said, pointing to the revolving front doors, "I could use some coffee, too."

The walk through the streets of lower Manhattan was an adventure. The mounds of garbage bags I saw along the streets last night were gone. They'd been cleaned up during the early morning hours. I watched cars dodging people who ran against traffic lights. Cab drivers either passed would-be passengers, or blasted their horns, and screamed obscenities at the rivals who had stolen their fares. Street vendors were setting up their counterfeit wares right in front of retail stores selling the real thing.

The morning rush hour crowds scurried into holes in the ground to be whisked off to who knows where. New Yorkers were lined up with cups of coffee in their hands, at newspaper stands, waiting to get their morning paper.

"Well," I quizzed Sam, "how was the midnight show?"

"You should have stayed," he said. "The entertainer did an impersonation of Elton John." Sam smiled, "Chris and I couldn't wait to get back to the hotel to ravage each other. Whenever we get away from Cincinnati, our sex life gets supercharged."

I winced. "I don't want to hear that shit, Sam. When I left your playground, I went back to the Sixth. I ran into an interesting character named Shudda."

Sam laughed. "The racetrack tout? He didn't give you any tips, did he?"

"Yeah, as a matter of fact, he did. The guy said our tattoo looked like the work of, wait a minute," I said, pulling out a notepad from my jacket pocket. "Let's see," I continued, turning a page on the pad. "Harry the Horse, Eddie the Mark, or Vinnie DeMilo."

"I don't know Harry the Horse. Vinnie is dead, I think. But I do know Eddie. He was on my beat when I worked the Sixth."

"How well do you know him? Can you believe him?"

"I know him, Jake, I didn't screw him. Eddie's a little outspoken maybe, but he's okay."

"Good then. Let's get started. We should be able to get all the information we need today and head home tonight."

Sam said, "I thought we'd go back home tomorrow."

"You just want to spend another night away from home with Christopher."

"No, that's not it. Chris is having dinner with one of his suppliers and asked if I'd join them. He's going back to Cincinnati in the morning, and I thought we'd go back together."

"Let's try to wrap this up today. I'm going to call Veronica, and maybe we can have dinner tomorrow night."

"You're feeling pretty good about yourself, aren't you?"

I pulled my cell phone out of my jacket pocket. "Yeah Sam, since I've gotten to know Veronica, I've had a new look at life."

*　　*　　*

We must have hit four or five tattoo parlors in Soho and Tribeca that morning. They didn't fit the profile. Most of the owners started their businesses a few years ago, but we questioned them anyway.

All these guys pointed us to Eddie and Harry.

Harry's place was the closest to the hotel, so we started there. Eddie's place was the furthest from the hotel, so Sam figured we'd save him for last.

Harry, the Horse, was cooperative, but he said it wasn't his type of work.

"I only do one-color drawings. It could be Eddie's work."

Harry suggested we check with the shops over on Canal Street in Chinatown. He told us there were a couple of places over on Eldridge Street that might do this kind of work and suggested we drop in on Eddie the Mark.

But first, Sam had to have his pastrami fix. He said the best deli in town was just up ahead and we could go to Chinatown after lunch.

92

"Sam, It's 11:20. Isn't it a little early for lunch?"

"We'll beat the crowd. The deli serves the best pastrami in New York. 'Eddie the Mark' can wait. The best deli is on Houston Street around the corner. I've been waiting two years to wrap my teeth around another one of *Katz's* pastrami sandwiches."

Sam was right. People were pounding down food as though the Russians were beating down the back door. The pickles were crisp and tart. The pastrami was sliced thin, and the sandwiches were four inches thick. The juices that filled my mouth when I bit into the sandwich ran onto my hands. Thank God I wrapped my napkin around my neck.

*   *   *

Almost every corner in Manhattan has a Sabrett hot dog stand. It's a place you can get a hot dog and drink for about five bucks. One sitting in front of The Rose Tattoo. The blue and yellow umbrella-covered stand served lunch to New Yorkers, on the run, juicy hot dogs covered with mustard, red onion, and tomato mix.

I would have tried one, but the pastrami sandwich did me in.

Eddie, the Marker Rose Tattoo, was a small artist parlor located on the ground floor of an old tenement building just across Canal Street in Chinatown.

The sign over the door read:
*The Rose Tattoo Offers World-Class Full
Custom Tattoos and Piercing.*

We stood in the doorway watching a tall skinny guy who could have danced through the Bengal's offensive line without being tackled. He was moonwalking to the driving beat of the *Bee Gees Staying Alive,* sucking down a bottle of Bud Light. He waved us in. The Barry Gibb wannabe didn't look the part. Eddie was a wiry man in his middle fifties. He was Six feet tall, completely bald, with a short salt-and-pepper beard. Bifocals that looked like they belonged on a university professor rested on the edge of his nose. His sleeveless tee shirt displayed red and green intertwined tattooed vines climbing up his bony arms and winding around his neck. A gold chain, with a Peace sign medallion, hung from his neck to the middle of his chest.

We walked into a large room lit up like an operating theater. High on the wall, behind the counter, hung a surveillance camera that watched over the drawings of multi-colored devil faces and skeleton skulls driving motorcycles hanging unframed on the walls. Padded chairs were positioned next to a table with a coffee cup and a half-eaten bagel.

"Sam," the tattooed man cried, wrapping his clinging vines around my partner. A wide grin spread across his face. "I thought I'd never see you again. Finally ready to dress up that great looking body?"

"No," Sam said, "we're here on police business." Turning to me, he said, "Say hello to my partner, Jake Laird."

"Is this the guy you followed to Ohio?"

"No, that's Chris. Jake's my street partner in Cincinnati. He's a cop, too."

Thank you, Sam.

I removed the picture of the killer's tattoo from my pocket, pushed the bagel and coffee aside, and laid it on the table.

"Eddie," I said, "we need some help finding the guy who drew this picture." Sam pulled his notepad and a Cross pen from his jacket pocket and began taking notes.

Eddie didn't even look at the picture. Instead, he walked away from me like his ass was on fire. I was right behind him.

"Hey, come back here. I asked if you knew who drew this."

"I don't know who drew this."

"I think you do."

"What part of *no* doesn't your partner understand, Sam?"

Sam's eyes hardened. "Don't be a wise guy." Sam placed his notepad down on the counter. "I know that look. You're hiding something."

Eddie listened, frowning, the scowl growing darker every second.

"Sam, I don't know who drew that. Try the guys over in Soho."

"We already did. The guys all said it's your work."

"I told you, I don't know who drew that."

Sam said. "Yes you do, Eddie."

"Stop harassing me. I told you don't know who did this drawing."

Sam said, "We're cops, Eddie, that's what we do."

Eddie's face drained of color. "Check with Vinnie DeMilo; this looks like his work."

"Eddie, Vinnie's dead."

"He probably did it before he died."

I asked, "Are you gonna get straight with me or am I going to have to give you a glass of smart water?"

Eddie put his head down and turned away.

"No, I told you I don't know who did this."

"Look, Eddie," I said, "We'll give you two ways to go. Tell us what we want to know, and it stays with us. Don't tell us and we will put it out on the street you did."

Bingo, I hit a nerve.

Eddie paused, walked over to the front door and turned the sign to Closed. He locked the door and motioned us to the back of the studio.

He ran his hand over his baldhead and stared at Sam a moment. "Come on; you live in Shitville. I live here. If I help you, and not Joey the Priest, whose dead body are they going to pull out of the East River?"

That was a surprise. Why did Eddie mention Joey Andronni?

Sam thought for a moment and said. "What's Joey got to do with this?"

"You're not going to like the truth."

"Then bullshit us."

It sounded like things were about to pop.

I grabbed the peace medallion hanging from his neck and yanked him toward me. "Eddie, don't lie to us or I'll stick my size eleven up your ass."

Another surprise was on the way.

"Two of Joey's goons showed me that same picture."

Pulling the photo from my hands, Sam stuffed it in Eddie's face. "This same photo?

"The very same."

Sam didn't have to say a word when he shot me a glance.

"Are you sure? Andronni's men?" Sam asked.

"Yeah, are there any other hairy gorillas with their knuckles dragging along Mott Street?"

Eddie spun away from me; walked over to the disc player, still blaring out another Bee Gees hit, and turned up the volume.

"Don't bullshit me," I said. "I think you know who drew this."

The disc hissed to an end. Eddie stopped and looked at Sam.

"Okay, okay," he said, looking around the room. "I did."

I eyed him warily. "You did this?"

Eddie reached over and picked up a stack of drawings. "Yeah, it has my mark right here, see?" Eddie was pointing to a tiny circle at the top of one of the drawings. He placed his index finger on the police photo. "See, it's here on the head of the Medusa."

I glanced at the drawings on the table.

Pay dirt. I was ecstatic.

"Did you tell them it was your work?"

He picked at a hole in his jeans. "No, you think I'm crazy? I told them it was Vinnie's work."

Sam jumped in. "Vinnie DeMilo is dead, remember?"

"I know that. Do you think I'm stupid? That's why I said he had to be the guy who drew it."

"And they believed you?" Sam asked.

Eddie cleared his throat. "The ape that went by the name of Bruno said if I were lying, they'd make my fingers look like yesterday's fucking beacon."

That rocked Sam back on his heels. "Are you saying Joey's people showed you this exact picture?"

Eddie scolded Sam. "What's the matter with your hearing, Sam? Same size, same paper. If you guys in Cincinnati are duplicating my work, you owe me royalties."

I was surprised by his answer: same size, and the same paper.

Tension filled the air. Sam was as hot as a match. "Don't be a wise guy, Eddie. It couldn't be the same. This photograph is from the Cincinnati police department."

"Well, so it seems, somebody in your squeaky clean police department is selling pictures to the mob."

I could see the fire in Sam's eyes. Suddenly we had another problem. Someone in the department was dirty.

I had to step in because Sam and Eddie looked like they were going to square off. "Tell me," I asked. "Who did you draw this on?"

"Lisa Turner, no Turheim. Turn-something. Shit, I don't remember her name."

"Don't you keep records on the work you do?"

"That was twenty-five years ago. I didn't keep records of the shit I did back then. Look around. Does this look like Merrill Lynch? Back then nobody kept real records in this business."

I told Eddie, "The tattoo business isn't exactly my forte. You must have drawn thousands of tattoos in twenty years. How can you remember work you did back then?"

He managed a tight smile. "You didn't see this broad. She had a set of Dolly Pardons that wouldn't quit. She wanted to have the figure put on each one with each nipple at each figures' mouth. She wanted those nipples to look like a tongue. Would you forget that? She said she wanted them to be different. I was itching to get my hands on those, but the guy she was with, who was paying for the work, wasn't buying it."

"So you settled for her leg?" Sam asked.

"I suggested I put it on cheeks of her ass. I told him he'd be the only one to see it."

"Both cheeks?"

"Just one."

"And, what'd he say?" I asked.

"The guy said she was a stripper in Atlantic City, so that wouldn't work."

Sam said, "So you put it on her leg? Didn't he think everyone would see it there?"

He shot Sam a cold look. "Sure, but the bastard grabbed me by the throat and convinced me it was in my best interest to find another place for the tattoo. That's when he showed me a nickel-plated knife That scared the shit out of me."

"How'd it get on her leg?" Sam asked.

"He told me to find another place or my ears and eyeballs would be on the floor."

"I was already losing my hair and didn't think it was time for me to go blind, so I suggested I put it there. Sam, the guy, was scary. I told him pointing to her boobs, who's gonna be looking at her legs?"

"What else can you tell us about her? What was her height, her weight? What did she look like?"

"She was about five-seven or eight, blonde hair, about a hundred and ten, hundred twenty pounds." Eddie paused, looked away and, shuffled his feet. He had the kind of body language that people use when they're not telling the truth. "She's a butter face."

I'd never heard that one before. It must be some New York saying.

"What's a butter face?"

"Great body, but her face is bad."

"Are you getting this down, Sam?"

"Yeah, Lisa Turner or Turkheim or something like that. She had a great body, but a bad kisser. She was a stripper on the Atlantic City boardwalk."

"And you told these goons the same thing," I asked, "minus the butter bullshit?"

"No, I only told them it looked like Vinnie's work, period."

I handed Eddie my business card and shot him a grateful smile. "Don't worry, this stays with us, and if anyone else comes in with a photo like this, tell them the Vinnie story and call me."

Just before the door clicked shut, Eddie called out, "Remember, I didn't tell you a thing."

"Don't worry," I told him. "We'll keep this in Shitville."

*   *   *

As we exited the shop, it began raining. I pulled up my collar.

"Now we're getting somewhere," Sam said. "We know part of the killer's name. There couldn't have been too many strip joints on the boardwalk back then."

"Not so fast, Sam. I'm not sure we should be sharing this information. It had to be someone in our precinct who passed the photo to Joey Andronni."

Sam looked across Canal Street at the heavy traffic to hail a cab.

"Why do you suppose Andronni's men are looking for this woman?"

"My guess is he wants to see what's on that flash drive," I said, "and if he's using his goons to find her, he probably wants some harm to come to her. What I'd like to know is how the hell Andronni got a hold of that photo?

A yellow cab screeched to a halt. Sam opened the front passenger door and flashed the driver his badge.

I opened the back door and climbed in. As we pulled away, I looked over my shoulder. There were two heavyset men, wearing dark, wraparound sunglasses and wide black-brim hats, standing under an umbrella alongside the hotdog stand, pounding down Sabrett hot dogs.

"A mole in the department. What the hell did we step into, Sam?"

"If Andronni is involved we'd better get to her before he does," Sam said. "Because if we don't, she's going to need a real priest."

Jake

Chapter 21

The return flight to Cincinnati was uneventful. Once we landed at the airport, I grabbed a cab back to the Cock N Bull where I'd left my car.

When I exited I-75, I drove past my old high school, Princeton High. That started my mind to wander from the case. When a man approaches his mid-forties, he's tempted to look back on his life. My father was killed in Viet Nam the day before I entered high school. Unlike my dad, my mom did see me graduate high school, but not college. Breast cancer took her and at age twenty I became an orphan.

Sam tells me the way my love life is going, the next person to see me naked will be a mortician. Thanks to Veronica it looks as though Sam's bullshit about my eventual exposure is circling the drain.

I thought of the soft kiss we had. Veronica didn't pull away. She smiled and left me with the words, "We don't have to go out. I can cook dinner at my place. There'll be time for us when you get back."

I needed to touch her. I wanted to hold her in my arms. I wanted to take her into my bedroom where our clothes would soon be on the floor.

*   *   *

I was at my desk at ten the next morning. Phil, the watch commander's assistant, requested a face-to-face meeting with Sam and me. I told him Sam was on his way.

"When he gets here," Phil said, "I want you both in my office." Around eleven my cell went off. I was hoping it was Veronica, but it was my partner.

Damn it. I've got to find another word for Sam.

"Jake," came his voice from the other end, "Eddie is in the hospital."

"Eddie who?" I asked.

"How many Eddies do you know?"

I thought for a moment, "Eddie the Mark?"

"That's right, Jake. DePasquale, the sergeant you met at the Sixth, just called. I gave him my cell number before I left."

I nodded, forgetting he couldn't see me. "Yeah, I remember him."

"A customer found him early this morning, sitting on a toilet seat with his pants around his ankles." Sam continued, "He had a hot dog, bun and all, stuffed in his mouth, the tomato and onion sauce running down his chin. They broke every bone in his body and pieces of his eyelids were on the floor. He took a hell of a beating, Jake. It looks like Eddie had the shit kicked out of him."

"Sounds like what an enforcer might do to get information.

"He's in the hospital, in a coma, Sam said. 'The doctors don't give him a chance to make it."

My mind shifted to the two guys, dressed in black, I had seen at the hotdog stand.

"You think Andronni's men came back?" I asked.

"Yeah, and it looks like the bastards try to pound him to death."

"Do you think he told them about us?"

"If they were watching the place, they saw us. My guess is whatever Eddie knew about Lisa; he tried to keep from them."

"Look, Sam, if he gave her up, they're coming to Cincinnati next," I said, looking at my watch.

"Why here?" Sam asked. "Don't you think she's left town?"

"Andronni knows Thompson bought it here, and if they got her address from Eddie, well, where would you start? Where are you?"

"At the airport. We just got in."

"I thought you were going to take the first flight out."

"Got up too late. Chris and I took the ten o'clock."

"See anyone on the plane that would fit the description of a couple of hoods?"

"No, most of the passengers looked like they were going to P&G or GE."

"As I said we took the ten o'clock. Maybe they took the earlier one."

"None of those guys work. They don't get up before noon."

"When's the next flight?"

Sam said, "Hold on, I'll check the arrival board. Most of the flights from New York are Delta's. Let's concentrate on them. The next one leaves New York at noon and gets in at two-thirty."

While Sam was checking, I shuffled the pages of the report we were going to turn in to Phil. I could hear him already. The artist who drew the tattoo was beaten up. How is that relevant? New York store owners get beaten up every day.

When you're trying to solve a cold-blooded murder, everything is relevant.

"Then there's another Delta flight at three-forty. They tell me there's non-stop from New York is an American flight. It comes in at five."

"Forget the five o'clock. Phil wants us to fill him in on New York. No sense you're waiting around the airport for three or four hours. I'll go back later. There's plenty of time to cover Delta's three-forty."

It was a long shot, I'll follow them. Hopefully, they'll lead me to Lisa.

*   *   *

Our meeting with Phil didn't go as smoothly as I would have liked. We filled him in on our visit with the tattoo artists we'd questioned, including Harry the Horse and Eddie the Mark. Sam told Phil that the sergeant at the Sixth Precinct called and reported that Eddie, one of the men we questioned, was severely beaten sometime last night.

Phil told us what had been going on with the Thompson case while we were in New York. He reached into the top drawer of his desk and threw out an edition of the *Cincinnati Enquirer.*

"They ran this yesterday," he said, pointing to the photo of the drawing on the killer's leg on the front page. "We're hoping someone recognizes the tattoo and gives us a name."

Sam thought for a moment. "Have you gotten any calls?"

Phil said, "The usual crazies. I've got Detective Phillips and her partner checking them out. One guy told us he killed a woman with a tattoo like that last week cause she wouldn't cook him his dinner."

"You didn't weed out the crazies?" I asked.

Phil's eyes narrowed. "We have to check out everything, even though that call came from Summit."

Sam asked, "The nut house?"

Phil shook his head and grumbled. "I can't believe they let the inmates use the phones."

All I wanted to do was get out onto the street and talk about this meeting over with Sam. I looked at my watch. "It's getting close to noon, Sam. Want to get a four-way?"

"You know chili, onions, and those red beans give me indigestion."

"Anything else?" I asked Phil.

"You guys haven't missed a thing, except we had another shooting in a downtown parking lot last night," he replied. "That makes four in the last three weeks. Here's the paperwork. Commander Cohen wants you to look it over."

"But Phil, we're working on the Thompson case."

"Put it on the back burner for a while. The mayor wants us to divert our attention to the tourists and citizens of Cincinnati."

"What bullshit," Sam complained. "This is an election year. I remember you telling us the mayor was concerned with visitors staying away from the downtown hotels."

Phil was adamant. "That was before we had this rash of shootings."

I picked up the file. "We'll look this over, boss."

"You better watch out, bad guys, here we come," I said, grabbing my coat and heading for the door.

Once outside Sam asked, "Any guess who the fink might be in the precinct?"

"Your guess is as good as mine. It could be anybody, but someone gave Andronni's people that picture. Until we find out who's dirty in the department, we're going to keep everything about this case to ourselves."

"Do you buy any of that crap from Phil?" Sam asked. "The tattoo killer is our case. Other detectives can get on the downtown shootings."

"Phil got his badge in a crackerjack box. Let's go through the motions of looking into these parking lot killings, Sam. I'm going out to the airport on my time. We need some eyeballs there. While you're at the airport, I'll make Westrope happy. While I'm there, you work the parking lot killings."

Sam said, "You might have to sit out at the airport for a few days."

"What's this *we* shit white man? We're both going to have to babysit these goons."

Chapter 22

Sam spent Tuesday afternoon at the Greater Cincinnati Airport. He called Al Scheff, a Boone County detective, and old golfing buddy. He asked Al for a copy of the passenger list from New York for the next few days.

Having worked in the Big Apple, the mob's backyard, Sam had a good handle on the kind of thugs we were looking for, but on his watch at the airport, nothing materialized.

Wednesday was my turn. When I got to the airport, Al was waiting for me.

"Hey, Jake," he said, standing on the curb. "I arranged a parking spot for you."

"Were you able to get a copy of the passenger lists for today's flights?"

"I called ahead," Al said. "They're like the ones I gave Sam yesterday. These are all of the flights coming in non-stop from New York today with the names of the passengers."

"All airlines?"

"All of them."

"Thanks, any problems getting them together?"

"No. What are you guys looking for?"

"A couple of goons. Sam didn't tell you?"

"No. All he said you guys were looking for a couple of thugs. All he asked me to do was to get the manifest for today's New York flights," Al said. He pointed to a uniformed guard who was walking toward us.

"Here comes security now." The guard managed a half smile, looked at Al and ignored me.

"This better be important, Al. The boss doesn't like stretching FAA rules."

"It's important," Al told the security guard. "Give Detective Laird all the help he needs. I gotta go, Jake. You guys owe me five strokes the next time we hit the ball."

"Deal, and thanks again for your help."

"Let's take this inside," the agent said, escorting me to an office alongside the escalators.

"Here's the manifest for all New York arrivals today," he said, handing me a three-page list when we arrived in the office. "Can I ask you what you're looking for?"

"Yeah, some thugs from New York."

"I'm not happy giving you this, especially without an officer from this county being present."

"I thought Detective Scheff cleared this with your people?"

"He did, but, as you can see, he left."

"Don't worry," I told the agent. "If they're the people we're looking for, I'm only going to follow them to Cincinnati."

"The next flight from New York is Delta's 6389. It's coming in at Gate B14."

"Thanks, and I appreciate your help."

I scrutinized the list. There were four passengers with names that ended with a vowel. We're taught not to profile, but two names jumped out at me, Bruno Ruggeri and Thomas Impelliteri. These two passengers were seated in 38A and 38B in the back section of the plane and likely would be among the last group getting off.

The passengers with Italian names could be a coincidence. Sam told me Joey Andronni had a reputation of bringing men, who spoke English, in from Sicily to do his dirty work. We were looking for a couple of killers and profiling was the best way to go. If the Israelis were successful doing it, then we weren't going to be politically correct either. I've learned that in this business, coincidences are the things you don't take for granted.

Across from Gate B14 was a glass-enclosed smoking area. I

stepped into the smoke-filled room. I'd rather chew on glass than to be in here, but its position in the terminal gave me a direct look at the exiting passengers.

The last two who came off the flight were wearing dark glasses. They were dressed differently than they had been the other day, but I was sure these were the pair I saw eating hotdogs in front of The Rose Tattoo.

Both men came off the flight with carry-on bags. They couldn't have gone through the screening machines in New York with weapons, so I was sure they weren't armed.

I was hoping they would walk by me and they did. Allowing a group of people to get between the two men and me, I grabbed the handrail and rode down to the tram that would take us to the baggage area.

When we got there, they went through the revolving doors and stepped outside onto the curb.

One of them removed a slip of paper from his coat pocket and unfolded it. He looked at the paper, took a cell phone from his pocket and ran his fingers over the keypad. I walked toward the Airport Security Officer standing next to my car.

"This yours?" He said pointing to my car.

"Yeah," I answered, showing him my badge.

I wanted to keep an eye on the suspects while continuing the conversation with the guard, but my attention was diverted to a black sedan with its hazard lights flashing that had pulled up to the curb.

The trunk of the sedan popped open, and the two guys tossed their bags into it and climbed into the back seat.

The sedan drove away. I fired up my engine and slowly pulled away from the curb.

Funny, the car looked like a county vehicle.

When I drove onto I-275, I picked up the two-way radio unit.

"Dispatcher, this is Detective Laird, District One. Please connect me to Detective Sam Ferris at one."

The voice came back. "Hold on I'll put you through."

It took only a moment. "Sam Ferris, may I help you?"

"Sam, it's me. I'm following an unmarked black Dodge Charger that looks like a Hamilton County car. The driver picked up those two goons from New York."

"What's the plate number?" Sam asked.

I pulled a little closer. "It looks like 76HAM77."

"Are you sure?"

"I'm positive. Why?"

"I don't have to check, Tracy. I know that number. It's one of ours."

Lisa

Chapter 23

I looked up from the computer screen. I kept telling myself not to panic, but if Andronni's men were looking for me, I was in big trouble. I should have sent him the flash drive.

This lousy tattoo was starting to feel like something stuck to the bottom of my shoe that I can't scrape off. I've got to leave town.

Nashville is about a five-hour drive from Cincinnati. I hadn't seen my friend Helen for two years, but I was sure she would let me hang out with her for a few days. My problem now was I had to figure out how I could use this flash drive to get myself out of this mess. Blackmail was the obvious answer, but I need to be careful. I've got to get away from Cincinnati like a chicken running from Colonel Sanders. If I don't, Joey the Priest will turn me into tenders.

I'd like to get word to Joey through Eddie to let him know I'd trade the drive for my life, but Eddie convinced me that wouldn't work. He said Joey's days of giving penance were over.

Yesterday, I went to the bank and closed my accounts. There wasn't much money left but was enough to get me to Music City. Joey's people had given my contact some up-front money for the hit on Hank, but most of that went for back rent on this house, my bookie, and the casino in Indiana.

It was spring in the Ohio Valley. Calm, clear skies. The sun beamed all day. The trees were growing greener by the day. I was looking forward to a pleasant drive down to the land of country music.

* * *

I snatched up the flash drive and placed it in my robe pocket. My suitcase was upstairs under the bed. I had to make sure I left nothing behind that would leave a trail.

I couldn't leave my cat, Miss Kitty. There was no one to take care of her. Helen doesn't have any pets. She doesn't like dogs, thinks they're too dirty. I couldn't leave her, so, I was banking on her liking my loveable kitty.

Looking out the window, I saw a black sedan pulled up in front of the house. Two guys dressed in black climbed out of the back seat. These two didn't look like Johnny Cash fans or Jehovah's Witnesses. One of the men directed the other to go around the back. They were Joey Andronni's men. I was sure of it. The one who was walking toward the back of the house stopped and stared at my car sitting in the driveway. The black sedan that brought them pulled away from the curb.

When I approached the stairs to go to my bedroom, Miss Kitty jumped onto the windowsill. She twitched her tail, arched her back, and let out a loud hiss. My grandmother called this move the 'Devil's Purr.' That put me on guard.

I went upstairs to get my nine-millimeter. When I got to the bedroom, I couldn't find the damn thing. It wasn't under the pillow where I usually kept it. I remembered it was in the desk drawer downstairs in the living room.

The front door was latched, and the patio door had a deadbolt. The kitchen door, the only one at the rear of the house, had a broken lock.

Miss Kitty was still on the windowsill downstairs. When I got to the top of the stairs, I looked down. I called her to me, "here Miss Kitty", but she didn't come. She continued to hiss loudly. I could hear the footsteps of one of the men coming up to the front door.

Now that I was upstairs, I was trapped. Staying in the bedroom wasn't an option. If this guy was one of Joey's men, the best thing for me to do was go back down and keep him off guard.

Suddenly there was a loud crash. The front door flew open. I heard a gun go off. Miss Kitty let out a loud hiss, but she didn't run up the stairs.

I came down the stairs and stood there staring at him. The big man wore a wrinkled black blazer over a grey tee shirt. His long black and grey hair tucked under a black hat. My blood froze at the sight of him standing at the foot of the stairs. He was unshaven and had dark wavy black hair. He had fury in his eyes. A wave of nausea crept up my throat.

"Who the hell are you?" I screamed.

His voice was deep and rough. "I'm da one who steps on worthless whores like you. Joey says hello."

"Where's my cat?"

"It's okay. I missed the lousy thing, but if you don't come down now, I'll kill it."

I started down the stairs slowly. My blood froze at the sight of the big man standing at the foot of the stairs.

The desk that held my nine was off to my right. If I went for it now, he was sure to block my path and blow my head off if I reached for it.

"Come down slowly," he said, waving what looked like a .357 Magnum.

I untied my robe, exposing my left side and one of my breasts.

He said, "Come a little closer and keep your hands where I can see them."

I scanned the room but didn't see my cat. Miss Kitty was probably hiding in her usual safe haven, underneath the sofa.

"What do you want?"

"To take a look at your leg."

"My leg? Why my leg?"

A sick grin spread across his face. "Don't give me that shit. You know why we're here. We want to see the tattoo."

"We?"

He waved the gun in my face. "My partner, Bruno, is in the back so don't get any idea's about running out on me. I want to see the tattoo your friend Eddie put on you."

My legs felt shaky. I drew a breath. Eddie wouldn't give me up.

"Eddie? Who's Eddie?"

"The guy who gave us your phone number. The rest was easy." He shook his head. I could see the frustration in his eyes. "Don't play games with me. Show me da leg."

I lifted my right leg and turned it toward him.

"That's nice," he said. "Now show me da other one."

I stepped toward him. I thought if I could get him to concentrate on the rest of my body, I should be able to catch him off guard.

I needed to show him I was scared. That might make him careless. I went into my crying act and started shaking my body.

"Where's my cat?"

He nodded. "At the other end of the living room. It ducked under da sofa. Stay back and show me your leg."

"Wouldn't you rather get your hands on these," I whispered, cupping both my breasts.

"Yeah, maybe later," he said with a smirk. "First, show me da other leg."

His attempt at a smile didn't convince me I'd be safe. I lifted my left side toward him and exposed the tattoo.

He raised his eyebrows. "Ah, there," he said, "Just where your friend said it would be."

"I don't believe Eddie told you where to find me."

"Well, like you, the tattoo guy thought he could bullshit us. But," he added, looking toward the back of the house, "not Bruno."

He shook his head and held out his fist to me. "See, your friend's' face messed up my hands."

The hairs on my arms stood up. "You beat it out of Eddie, didn't you?"

My heart was racing. Tears began rolling down my cheeks, but this time they were real. I had to get a hold of myself.

"You're crying. That's nice. He was loyal to you. You should have heard him crying while we kicked da shit out of him. Bruno broke a couple of his fingers and knocked out most of his teeth. He didn't give you up until we cut out one of his eyelids."

He took his eyes off my leg and stared at my breasts.

Holding them I asked, "Wouldn't you like to get a hold of these?"

"After you give me da thing you took from the guy you whacked."

"What thing?"

"Don't act dumb. Where is the thing you were supposed to send to New York."

"No, I don't. I've got the tattoo you're looking for, but that's it."

"Look, we don't want to spend a lotta time in this town. Give us da thing we came for and then I'll let you go."

Ignoring this gorilla, I said, "I told you, I don't know what you're talking about."

"Look, you have two choices, I can kill you, or something else can happen. You don't want to end up like your friend Eddie, do you? One way or the other, we're ain't leaving here without da thing we came for."

"We?"

"Let me call my friend, Bruno," he said, looking toward the back of the house.

I dropped my head. It was useless to argue with this dip-shit. His friend Bruno was probably an animal too.

"It's in the kitchen, on the counter."

"Show me and don't get any funny ideas." He grabbed my forearm like a wrestler about to hurl his opponent across the ring.

"Be nice, sweetheart. I won't kill you until after I screw you."

"You said you'd let me go if I gave you what you want."

"I lied, but only about letting you go. I'm still planning on doing you."

Good, now the son of a bitch was talking my language. I ran my hands down his chest and dropped to my knees and started to unbuckle his belt.

I've learned you can always count on a man's small head screwing up the reasoning of the big one.

"Later," he said. "First get me da thing we came for."

"Come on handsome," I told him, pushing a smile to my lips. I started to rub my hands over his crotch. "Let me have some fun, now."

He placed the barrel of the silencer and moved it along the side of my face. I looked up at the fire of his stare.

He winked at me. "Okay, go ahead, help yourself," he said, "but remember what we're here for."

"I'll give you the thing after you get your rocks off. Call your friend in," I told him. "I like to do two at a time."

"No," he said, sticking his groin into my face. "Bruno," he said laughing, "He doesn't like broads."

He unzipped his pants and put the gun down on the kitchen counter, wrapped his hands around the back of my head.

He was holding me so tight I felt like gagging. After a while, I could feel his body starting to stiffen.

"Hang on baby, here I cum," he cried.

I smiled and looked up at him. I bit down hard, hoping to inflict as much pain as possible.

He screamed, his dark eyes smoldering.

I didn't dare let go. I started twisting my head from side to side and kept my teeth clamped hard.

His scream was so loud I couldn't believe the guy outside hadn't come to his rescue.

He pounded the side of my head with both his hands.

"Whore!" He kept screaming. He continued to beat my head with his hands wrapped in a ball. Like a rock, I dropped to the floor.

He went to one knee, grabbed me by my neck, and hurled me across the kitchen floor.

I got to my feet, wiped drips of blood and semen off of my lips, and sprinted for my desk and the nine-millimeter.

"Bitch," he yelled one hand on his crotch, the other hand grabbing the gun off the kitchen counter. He fired off a round that whistled past and embedded itself in the sofa.

When I reached my desk, I opened the top drawer. The nine-millimeter Glock was there.

"Get on your knees, bitch," he cried.

I dropped to my knees and looked away.

"If you're going to kill me, let me stand," I pleaded, getting back on my feet.

He yelled, "Get back on your knees!"

"Fuck you," I told him. "I've been on my knees or my back all of my life. I'm not going to die this way."

"After what you did to me, I should let Bruno come in, pull out your eyes, and slit your throat!"

I had one last chance. "It's in here," I told him, pointing to the open top drawer. I stood up slowly and positioned myself in front of the desk so he couldn't see the Glock. I placed my hand on the drawer handle.

"Leave it. I'll get it after I whack you."

He pointed his gun inches from my forehead.

"Turn your head to the side, bitch."

"No, if you're going to kill me do it now."

I looked past him. Miss Kitty slinked out from under the sofa. She raised her tail, lashing it back and forth. She hissed loudly. Arching her back high into the air, she spat and pounced toward him.

That's when he made his last earthly move. Startled by the sound of Miss Kitty, his head jerked to the side. He spun around, looked over his shoulder, and hesitated.

I grabbed my nine from the opened desk drawer, raised the Glock and blew his fucking head off.

Jake

Chapter 24

I was a full block behind the black Charger when it turned the corner and disappeared. I've never been in this section of the city before.

Although it was an old residential area, I was surprised to see there were only three houses on this street. The rest of the street had empty lots with 'For Sale' signs.

"Where are you, Sam? I need backup." I could hear the wailing of his siren through my two-way radio.

"I had to stop at the motor pool to change a tire. I'm on my way," he explained. "I'm on I-75. I know the area. I'll exit at Galbraith Road. I should be there in a couple of minutes. Where are you?"

"On Compton Avenue. When you get off, 75 go to Vine and take a right on Vine. There's a BP station on the south corner and a *Penn Station* sandwich shop on the northwest corner of Compton. Take a left. Call Phil and have him get with the local guys, so they know we're here."

I reminded Sam to cut the siren.

"There're only a few houses on this street. This looks like a new development. I'm going to drive to the end of the street and turn around. I can get a better look at the houses from the driver's side."

Sam asked, "Where's the county vehicle?"

"It's gone. It must have dropped those guys off and left."

I removed my sunglasses and looked up at the door wide open on the first house on the block. "Wait," I said. "There may be something going on in the house on the corner. Check this out: 3956 Compton. Check and see who lives there."

I doubled back, stopped my car, and looked up at the two-story structure.

As much as I wanted to go in, I couldn't. I needed probable cause to enter a private residence. We didn't have a warrant. We didn't even have a reason to get one.

I can hear the DA now. "What law did the men you were following break? Were you following them because they exceeded the speed limit? Maybe these guys were meeting with a friend. Maybe they were delivering flowers to a grieving family member. You've got to give me more."

But that was bullshit. We were investigating a murder. Maybe the person who lived at 3956 Compton was our killer. Maybe the guys in there were paying her off or tying up loose ends.

I couldn't sit there forever, but then again, without a warrant, I had to.

These were the goons who nearly beat Eddie to death. I guess that Lisa-something could be in for the same fate.

What could I do?

My mouth felt like the Gobi desert. I reached into the cup holder, took out a can of *Red Bull*, opened it and took a sip. I looked out the car window.

Then it hit me. Exigent Circumstances, that's it. I could use this law if I felt there was an imminent danger to life or property. I decided to go in.

I called Sam back, "I'm going in. Exigent Circumstances should give me probable cause. These bastards are probably armed. Put on your vest," I told him. "I'm getting out of the car and putting on mine."

After I put on the vest and adjusted it, I drew my Glock and clicked the safety off. I placed my badge on the vest and started up the stairs. The door was open ajar. That's when I heard gunfire.

The adrenaline surged through my body. I reached the top of the steps, swallowed real hard, stepped inside, and scanned the room.

A blonde in a robe was standing, in the living room, over a body. His penis was bloody and standing at attention. A cat was spitting at me. Arching its back, it jumped toward me.

I flashed my badge, but evidently, the cat didn't give a shit and the animal kept on spitting.

I yelled at the blonde. "Cincinnati police Lisa, drop your weapon."

She looked across the room and cocked an eye toward me. She started to lower her weapon when the back door flew open. The guy burst into the room as though his ass was on fire. He must have been in the back when his partner got his head blown off. He heard the shot and assumed his partner had whacked the blonde.

The man, bursting through the door, was short and stocky. He raised his pistol and started firing. "Say your prayers cause," he shouted, "you're fucking dead." Then ping, ping, ping, the chilling sound of the ejecting shells hitting the wooden floor.

The bottom fell out of my stomach. I stumbled forward, ducked behind an overstuffed chair, and started firing. The blonde wheeled and started emptying her nine at him. He ducked behind the refrigerator. Her helping me didn't last. She stopped firing. Her clip was empty. She threw the gun aside and grabbed her purse sitting on the desk. Grabbing the cat she tucked it under her arm and flew past me.

She raced out the open front door and looked back over her shoulder.

Her eyes glazed over. "See ya!" she hollered, "the fucker's all yours."

She ran through the door and down the steps. A few seconds later I could hear a car screeching out of the driveway. It had to be hers. She must have left ten pounds of rubber in the driveway.

I popped up from behind the stuffed chair and squeezed off a few rounds. Bullets whizzed over my head.

With her gone, he started firing at me. My heart pounded. I

squatted as deeply to get as much leverage out of my legs as possible. I reached down, placed both hands at the bottom of the stuffed chair, and heaved it at the eighteen-wheeler coming at me.

He sidestepped the chair and turned his attention to the front door; not at the fleeing blonde, but at Sam, who had delayed a second before charging in, pistol raised, his vest strapped to his body.

In that second, the gunman fired away at the open door. Sam fired all nine shots of his service weapon. They hit the ceiling, the bookshelves, floor-everything but the gunman.

One of the goon's bullets cut into Sam's neck. The impact of the shells tearing into his vest sent him backward. The pops on his chest and neck were sickening. He bounced against the wall and slid over on his side. The bastard kept firing. I aimed, and emptied my nine into his chest.

My heart sank. Sam wasn't moving. I got down on my knees beside him.

"Officer down!" I screamed into my two-way phone. "Officer down! 3956 Compton Street, Wyoming. Officer down! I need a bus. Hurry, God damn it! Hurry!"

I placed Sam's head in my lap. There was so much blood it was like a fresh spring sprouting from his neck. I placed my thumb on the wound hoping to stem the flow, but it spread over my hand and knees forming a puddle around them. I pulled out a handkerchief and wiped his face. His lips were turning blue. He was turning cold and clammy. I was shaking. Tears ran down my cheeks.

"Hang in there, Sam, help's coming." I looked up at the ceiling and whispered, "please, God, don't take my partner."

Jake

Chapter 25

The paramedics wouldn't allow me to sit in the back of the ambulance with Sam. They could see I was upset and figured I'd get in the way.

The rain was falling as I followed, siren blaring, weaving through the late afternoon traffic on I-75. I called Division 1 and requested a department presence at University Hospital.

At the stroke of four on this rainy, on this April day, amidst shouting reporters, I pulled through the ER's circular drive.

The paramedics hustled Sam through the doorway of the emergency room. I wiped my brow and got out of the car. I wanted to walk, but ended up sprinting, avoiding the puddles in the driveway toward the large oversized doors leading to the emergency room.

Herman Williamson, the city beat writer from *The Cincinnati Enquirer*, ran across the parking area waving his arms trying to get my attention.

"Jake!" he called out. "It just came over the scanner officer down. It's not Sam, is it?"

I turned my back, but he caught up with me.

"Not now, Herman."

"How bad is it?"

Like most newspaper reporters, Herman could be a pain in the ass, but unlike most of these clowns, he cared.

"I don't know yet. If you get the hell out of my way, we'll both find out."

I pushed my way past TV camera operators hustling to set up their equipment outside the entrance.

I kept thinking that even though he was wearing his vest, he still got hit. He broke rule number one; walk, don't rush to your death. What the hell are the odds of getting shot in the neck? Why wasn't it his leg or his arm? should have waited for Sam and backup to get there before I went in. Who cared if that thug cut down Lisa? That would have been the end of the case.

My problems seemed a million miles away. The breakup with Carol, the new relationship with Veronica, they were all meaningless. Suddenly it dawned on me, Sam, no, my *partner* Sam, could die.

As I went through the entrance to the ER one of the nurses grabbed me by the arm and led me into the casualty department.

Casualty department. That's what the guys in homicide call the ER. It didn't seem funny anymore. The depressing walls of the hospital and the broad seal of the city of Cincinnati and the mayor staring me in the face didn't make it any easier to think positively about my partner.

The crowd inside was as hectic as the media circus outside. It was with good reason another ambulance had just delivered victims from a multi-car crash on Martin Luther King Drive.

Nurses were attending to the victims. They were checking blood pressure readings, temperatures, and registering pulses. Bandages wrapped around the arms and legs of patients and wheelchairs pushed through the wide swinging doors that led to the emergency room.

The speaker shrieked a code blue.

Was that for Sam? I pushed my way through the crowd and grabbed the first nurse who walked by. I shoved my badge in her face.

"I'm with the Cincinnati police. Was that code blue for the police officer brought in?"

She looked at my pants and hands, soaked with blood.

Taking my arm, she led me to toward the ER. "You're bleeding sir, please let me help you."

"No, no, I'm fine," I told her, "It's not my blood."

She hesitated, before speaking, staring at my gold badge. "The accident on Martin Luther King Drive. Were you involved with that?"

"No, the detective that was brought in here with a gunshot wound. Do you know where he is?"

"He's in the ER." She pointed to the desk with the sign over it marked Admissions. "Maybe they can help you. That blood looks heavy; you better have your legs looked at."

Walking up to the admissions desk, I put my identification to work. "My name's Detective Laird. The police officer just brought in here, where is he?"

The clerk stood up and grabbed my badge and pulled it to her face to get a better look, I guess. "Do you see what's going on around you? We're busy." She pushed the badge back to me.   "

"You're with the Cincinnati police?"

"Yeah, where's Detective Ferris?"

"Good," she said, chomping down on her gum. "We need more information about the policeman."

"He's a Cincinnati, police officer."

She shook her head and looked at her computer screen. "We know that, sir. The paramedics called telling us there is a policeman with a gunshot wound being rushed here."

She asked me if I was family and wanted to know Sam's age, and whether the information the hospital had on the Cincinnati police insurance was up-to-date.

"He's my partner," proud to say it, not caring how she took it.

"He's forty-five. Who cares about insurance? The City of Cincinnati insures him."

"His partner?"

"Yes, you know," I said cocking my head and smiling, "We're life partners." I can't believe I said that, but if telling her I was his partner would get me the information I needed, I didn't care what the hell she thought.

She wrinkled her forehead. "Oh, I'm sorry. I didn't mean to pry. Who's the carrier? Our records show Blue Cross covers police."

"Yeah, Blue Cross, Red Cross, double cross, who cares. Why do you have to know that now?"

"We need to develop a medical record."

"Where did they take him?"

"They took him into the trauma center. Doctor Bennett is the trauma surgeon on duty today."

She pointed to the glass-enclosed waiting room across from her desk. "Please wait there. The doctor will be out as soon as they're finished."

What was Sam's condition? Where the hell was Doctor Bennett?

My philosophy on doctors is simple. When they give you a concerned look and tell you to sit down, it meant only one thing. They were about to lay some bad news on you.

"Since you're his life partner, Doctor Bennett will want to speak to you."

Partner. That's when it hit me. Christopher. How was I going to get word to him? Did I have Sam's home number in my cell? I was looking for it when all hell broke loose.

Scurrying through the TV reporters, like rodents, were the Mayors of Cincinnati and Wyoming, the police chief of Wyoming, Cincinnati's police chief, Arthur Cole. Cole is the head of the FOP, Samuel Ramsey, and of course, Commander Ed Cohen.

Reporters were jockeying for position to shove their microphones In the faces of anyone who moved through the reception area. Cincinnati's Chief of Police was the first to be interviewed, followed by the mayor. Face on the nightly news was the only thing these guys were interested in. None of them, including the head of the police union, bothered to find out Sam's condition or who was taking care of him. I wondered how they got here so fast.

Was it the accident on Martin Luther King? The call I made, saying an officer was down, must have set them in motion.

In the waiting room people looking at the TV screen. The television interviews were going on less than fifty feet away. I pushed my way through the crowded room. My blood was boiling. I wondered when the hell this group would get around to asking about Sam's condition.

I needed to go to the restroom and clean up. I had Sam's blood on my hands, but I didn't dare leave. It would be my luck the doctor would come looking for someone from Sam's family while I was gone.

I felt nauseous. I sank down in a black chair and glanced at the clock on the wall. I grabbed a magazine and thumbed through it. What the hell was I doing? I couldn't concentrate on anything but Sam and the whereabouts of Doctor Bennett. I took a deep breath, threw the magazine aside, got up and started to pace about the room. What was I going to tell Christopher?

Then the second wave of nausea and anxiety hit me. I froze when I saw a man dressed in blue scrubs walking toward the waiting room. I eyed his tall, lanky frame. He was in his late forties, with a gray-streaked beard. He removed his blue cap and ran his hand through his graying hair. He wasn't smiling.

He opened the door and stepped into the waiting room. "I'm Doctor Bennett," he said. "I'm looking for anyone from Mr. Ferris's family."

My nerves shot to the outer layers of my skin.

"That would be me, Doctor. Jake Laird, I'm his partner."

"Your legs are covered with blood. Let me get you to the trauma center."

"The blood's not mine. It's your patient's."

He shook my hand and looked down at his feet.

His words were painful. "Mr. Ferris's condition is critical." He placed his hand on my shoulder. "The vest he was wearing kept the bullets from entering his chest. It's the neck wound that concerns us. He's lost a great deal of blood. We've been able to stabilize him," he said with a grim shake of his head.

I started to ask about Sam's prognosis, but a lump jammed my throat. I remained silent. I couldn't breathe. We just stood there staring at one another. My heart was pounding.

"He is going to make it, right?" I asked.

Dr. Bennett looked at me with tired eyes. "You better sit down," he said, pointing to the chairs along the wall. "The bullet just missed the carotid artery in his neck. That's the main artery that

124

leads to the brain." Bennett looked away. "Your partner is fighting for his life. He's in a coma."

I stared at Bennett. The hairs on the back of my neck stood erect. The doctor's next statement felt like a sharp elbow jammed in my gut.

"The next forty-eight hours are critical. You'd better call his family."

That's when I realized what being Sam's partner meant. I was his family.

Chapter 26

Commander Cohen looked like an undertaker in his shiny black suit, white shirt, and a large black tie. Given the circumstances, his look wasn't understanding.

The seal of the city of Cincinnati, pictures of President Obama, Mayor Bergman, Governor Kasich, and Police Chief Harrington hung behind his desk scowling down at me between the Stars and Stripes and the state flag of Ohio. Cohen didn't take his eyes away from mine, and said, "What the hell were you thinking, Laird?" He looked down at his desk and consulted a folder. He looked up, stared at me, and started shouting. "You decided to take on two hit men from New York, alone?"

I placed my face in my hands and asked myself over and over again the same questions. Should I have requested backup from the Wyoming police? That would have been another way to attack the problem. Was I trying to be too macho?

A shiver went through me. "I didn't go in until after I heard a gunshot. What would you have me do?" I said, getting up from my chair. "Play with myself until the posse came to my rescue?"

"I didn't expect a Dirty Harry imitation. Sit back down, detective."

His dark eyes smoldered. "You should have thought of that before you ran in there, guns blazing. You're in big trouble. The chief is looking into your jacket, and if he finds a DUI or even a twenty-year-old parking ticket, you'll be behind a desk until they find Jimmy Hoffa. As of this moment, you're on suspension."

I glared at Cohen. A force took hold of me. "This is bullshit," I said. "It's total crap. For doing my job?" He was daring me to make a case out of charging in without the backup.

"No, Laird. When you call and ask for backup, and in this case you did, it means you're supposed to wait. You're making this division look bad."

I swiveled back and forth in the chair before responding. "I know what I'm doing. I'll do my job and make decisions depending on what the situation on the ground is."

"You'll do it by the book, detective, or someone else will."

I knew what this meant. Cohen was going to shift control on the case, my case.

"That's not fair, commander. You bring my ability into question every time Phil Westrope sits me down and reads me your riot act."

Cohen turned his attention to the outer office. "Doctor Mendenhall is waving a file at you. Now get the hell out of my office. I want your paperwork handed into Lieutenant Westrope before you leave tonight. With your partner down you're going to sit this one out."

Veronica to the rescue.

I tried not to show my outrage. Westrope was the boss. I didn't know the bastard very well, but my guess is the only time he spent on the job was identifying hookers and petty crooks. He'd probably never seen the business end of a Glock.

I pulled in a deep breath of the not so fresh air and walked out of his office.

"Jake," Veronica said, grabbing my hand and squeezing it. "I called the hospital, but you had already gone. I didn't get to speak to the attending physician," she paused, looking at her notepad, "Dr. Bennett."

"It's a neck wound. Sam's lost a lot of blood, but he's hanging in there."

"I got that much from the trauma nurse on duty," Veronica continued. "I left a message for Doctor Bennett to call."

"The bastard couldn't have missed. I was behind a stuffed chair, and Sam was coming through the door."

She gripped my hand tighter. "You did all you could. Sam followed procedure. His vest was on, and he got hit in his neck."

"I know I should have waited, but I couldn't tell Cohen I was wrong to go in without back-up."

She shook her head. "I don't blame you for not telling him. Your admission is safe with me. In fact, I like you better for admitting you're not perfect."

"I didn't figure Cohen would chew me out while Sam is fighting for his life." I leaned over my desk and buried my face in my hands again. "I need some fresh air. Let's step outside."

"I almost forgot," Veronica said, handing me a folder. "Medford says the woman's gun left behind, in Wyoming, is the gun that killed Thompson."

"I'm not surprised."

"But, it's not the murder weapon for the guy in Norwood."

"A copycat?" I barely got the words out of my mouth when the door to Phil's office swung open. He came out of his office calling my name, and he wasn't alone. There was walking behind him who looked familiar.

"In my office, Jake. Excuse me, Doctor Mendenhall, I need to speak to Detective Laird."

"I'm working on the report now, Phil," I said. "I'll have it for you before I leave tonight."

"You might not leave tonight," Phil replied, "You do know Sam's partner, Christopher Epstein?"

"No. We've talked on the phone, but we've never met."

"Let's go into my office, Laird."

"I'll look this over," I said to Veronica placing the file under my arm. "I'll get back to you."

Veronica touched me gently on the shoulder before moving away.

I pulled a water bottle from my jacket pocket and popped a couple of aspirins. I was hoping it would head off the headache I knew Phil was about to give me.

"What's this Detective Laird bullshit, Phil?" I asked.

Then it struck me. I looked at Christopher.

I said, "You're the guy who was dressed in a tuxedo, who let the

Elton John impersonator into the club in New York the other night."

He stepped toward me; his voice filled with contempt. His eyes looked at me with a flash of sudden fury. "Yes, and you're the asshole who got my Sam shot!"

What the hell was he doing here? I hadn't seen that one coming. He should be at the hospital with Sam.

"Shouldn't you be with Sam in the hospital?"

"They're not allowing visitors. His condition is critical."

That's when Phil stuck his finger in my face. "You, follow me."

Phil asked Christopher to wait outside. "I know you want to get in touch with the hospital. Mr. Epstein, please feel free to use the phones."

When we reached the office, Phil held the door open and pointed to the chair across from his desk. I stepped inside. After I sat down, Phil turned, closed the door, folded his arms, and looked at me.

"I've got good news and bad news." He cleared his throat. "Which one do you want to hear first?"

My eyes met his eyes. "Just tell it."

"The good news is the hospital called. They were able to stabilize him."

What a relief. Mentally I made the sign of the cross. Thank you, God.

"He's out of danger?"

"No."

"What's the bad news?"

"The bad news is something you already know. Why haven't you and Sam said anything about the mole in this office?"

My knees went weak. That came out of the blue. If it had been a right cross, it would have been a knockout and put me flat on my back. I glanced anxiously around the room as though looking for someone. "A mole? What the hell are you talking about?"

Phil was silent for a moment. "The dirty cop you and your partner conveniently left out of your New York report. Listen, Laird. I'm...."

I interrupted him. "Where the hell did you hear that?"

Phil looked out over the squad room. Mendenhall had already left. Christopher was the only one in the outer office. He was sitting at Sam's desk; phone in hand, dialing a number.

Phil was silent and then said, "Him," he said pointing to Christopher.

I sat there dumbfounded. "Sam's Christopher?"

Phil looked directly into my eyes. "Sam told him, in New York those hit men were one step ahead of you."

"Some grief-stricken guy comes in here and gives you some crap about a mole in our department, and you believe him?" I asked.

"Pillow talk."

"Bullshit," I told him in my best screw-you voice. "Phil," I continued, "if I thought we had a dirty cop in the department I'd tell you."

Phil shrugged. "There's only one reason why you didn't tell me. For Christ's sake, Laird, you think it's me."

"No, I don't, but let's assume you're right about a mole." I reminded Phil, "If your Mr. Epstein out there tells Cohen or anyone else about what he told you, the guy is toast."

"Why is that?"

"He's a civilian. Suppose he goes to the press? That will bring on an investigation."

Phil was adamant, "First, tell me whatever you know about this dirty cop theory of yours."

"First, promise me you'll assign a guard outside of Sam's room at University Hospital until he's moved."

"We'll see, but what about him?" Phil asked, motioning to Christopher.

I said, "You'd better have a long talk with him, or he'll need a guard too."

"I'll have to get the paperwork okayed by Cohen."

"Bullshit, Phil, I've seen you forge his signature before. If Christopher has it in for me, he has it in for the whole department."

"What are you getting at?"

"Don't you think, whoever the mole is, he's going to want to keep his identity a secret?"

"You're probably right, Laid. No leaks," Phil warned me, "Everything you find comes through me. No contact with your friend from the *Enquirer.*"

Phil kept his face expressionless. "Okay. Now tell me what else have you've got."

"Take a look at the motor pool and see who's assigned a black Dodge Charger license number 76HAM77."

Phil's head drooped slightly.

"Are you sure of that number?"

"Yes, I am."

"It's Cohen's."

Chapter 27

Commander Ed Leonard Cohen believes politicians and thieves are liars by nature.

When he first joined the Cincinnati Police Department, the young Cohen vowed to put all the enemies of the city and state behind bars. He was known for his ability to wrap a guy up into a pretzel real fast.

After a few years on the job, he began to lose his faith in the law.

He told his partner, Charlie, "I put the bastards behind bars, and their wise-ass attorneys get them off because I may have smacked their clients around a bit. Those shysters write the laws that make it difficult for prosecutors to convict criminals. This job is turning into bullshit."

Early in his career, he and Charlie arrested two wanna-be gangbangers. The older suspect had a 'who gives a shit' attitude. Detective Cohen had never questioned him before.

The younger suspect didn't have a record and could not have known he'd be in for a painful night.

The two had held up a young couple in a downtown Cincinnati parking lot, and the younger thief kept the male victim's wallet.

"I was going to get their phone number, call them, and tell them I found their wallet," the thief told Cohen.

Cohen's partner, Charlie laughed. "You're supposed to take the money and dump the evidence before you get caught. Didn't they teach you anything in crime school?"

Without warning, Cohen lashed out and pounded the older man in the face with his wooden baton, breaking his nose. His face smeared with blood, he fell limp hitting the floor.

"How are we going to question him now, Ed?" His partner Charlie asked. "He's a mess."

Cohen smiled in a fractured sort of way. "I don't want to talk to him." He pointed his baton to the other suspect. "I want to talk to this guy. Now listen, kid, you won't be able to help your friend if you're lying next to him. It would look funny to have both of you going to the hospital together. It's a lot of paperwork for me so let's not waste any of my fucking time, okay?"

The coffee-skinned suspect stared at Cohen.

"I'm not afraid of you," he said, looking away from Cohen.

Cohen's eyes widened. "You're not? Then you're dumber than you look. You should be terrified. Take a look at your friend. I'm just getting started."

Cohen raised his foot and brought it into the fallen man's ribs. "See, I'm trying to wake him up."

The young man thought for a moment. His choice was hard but simple. He looked down at his fallen partner's bloody face. "Then I guess I'd better not waste your time."

"Good," Cohen said, handing him a yellow legal pad and a pencil. "I want to know who did what. Write it all down. You can write, can't you?"

"Yes, sir."

"Ya see, Charlie," Cohen said to his partner, waving his baton over the guy passed out on the floor. "It's not what or who you ask," he paused, "It's how you ask it.

Chapter 28

Joey Andronni's long black Lincoln snaked its way through the dense, Manhattan mid-town evening traffic. His car eased to a stop in front of his favorite Manhattan steak restaurant, his cell went off.

"It's for you, boss," Paulie said, his hand over the receiver.

"Who is it?" Andronni asked.

Paulie opened the door and thrust his heavy frame onto the sidewalk. His eyes swept their immediate surroundings for suspicious characters loitering in doorways. Seeing none, he motioned his boss out of the Lincoln and handed him the cell phone. "It's that senator from Illinois."

Andronni grunted. "Tell him I'm sitting down to eat, and I'll talk to him when I'm good and ready."

"He doesn't have time for you now," Paulie barked into the cell. "He'll call you back when he wants to talk to you."

Paulie walked toward the restaurant and started to snap the phone shut. Suddenly, he brought it back to his ear.

"What'd you say?" Paulie cried out. "They're what? They're dead?"

He turned and stared at Andronni. "Boss, I'm afraid you're going to have to take this."

Andronni grabbed the phone, took a deep breath and shouted into it. "My friend, don't you know it's not wise to bother a man when he's sitting down to eat? Please tell me you have the goods."

Andronni paused; his eyes opened wide, his lips curled in anger. He ignored the pedestrians staring at him as they passed. "Are you telling me the men I sent to Pisstown are dead? You do have what they went after, don't you?"

Andronni walked back to the car, seething. He pressed the cell to his ear. When he reached the Lincoln, he gulped in the night air, opened the back door, climbed in, and sat down.

Paulie slammed the car door shut. Joey began screaming at the top of his lungs. "I thought the help you were getting from those cops was going to put this broad in the ground and end this game." Joey wouldn't let up. "So what you're telling me is your people picked up my men at the airport and drove them to get whacked?"

"They picked them up and took them to the hitter's house," Morrison answered. "The woman killed one of your men. A Cincinnati detective shot the other."

"I don't give a shit who killed who, friend. My men are dead, right?"

"Yes, they're both dead."

"And they're not coming back, right?"

"Yes."

"Then I'm out two men, right?"

"Well, I wouldn't put it that way."

"Excuse me, my friend, for interrupting, but how else would you put it? What was your connection, with the local police doing, while my people were getting whacked?"

"He's with the Cincinnati police and couldn't run the risk of showing himself. The plan was to give them the weapons, take them to the address we gave him and return when your men completed the job. He didn't know they were being followed."

Andronni as was as was as hot as a match. "He's a fucking cop, and he doesn't know he's being followed? Who the hell did you send, Stevie Wonder?"

"This is just a bump in the road," Morrison said. "We'll get her."

"Bump in the road? I don't see any bumps in *my* fucking road, my friend. So now the cops have two dead men who can be traced back to New York and maybe my organization. One of those men I brought in from Sicily. The other was violating his parole. He wasn't supposed to leave the state of New York." Andronni paused for a moment to come up for air. "We look like Moe and Larry here. Now, all we need is fucking Curly to show up. I'm beginning to feel like you and the broad you hired, to whack Hank, have shoved us into quicksand."

"I told you, Joey, I didn't hire her, but we'll get her. We just ran into a bit of bad luck."

Andronni ignored him. He's heard those types of excuses a thousand times before. Usually, men who didn't get a job done disappeared.

"Look, friend, we're not sure what's on that flash drive. If it contains information on the money we funneled to you for your election or your Thailand operation, your connections will throw you under the bus, and we'll all end up rotting in federal prison."

"I'm sure Hank wasn't stupid enough to keep the records of our operations on his computer."

"You'd better hope he wasn't that dumb. Do you even know where this broad is? How the hell are you going to get her? You guys in Washington couldn't find your ass with both hands tied behind your back."

"Don't worry. We'll get her and the flash drive."

Andronni climbed out of the limo and looked at his driver leaning against the car. Paulie's eyes were on fire. He had lost two men in his crew. There was nothing he could do about it.

"Senator, one of my rules is you don't throw away your dirty water until you get clean." He paused, hoping to let the statement sink in. "And your fucking water, my friend, is beginning to look like shit. We got Jack Kennedy remember? And he had an army of bodyguards. Senator, if you don't clean up this mess, the next thing you lose won't be an election."

*　*　*

Senator Morrison hung up the phone in his Chicago office. It didn't matter to Joey Andronni that he was talking to a United States

Senator. Morrison made the call to Andronni because he thought it was best to let the thug blow off some steam, but Joey was right. It was the senator's fervent belief that they had to get to the hitter and the flash drive or they could all go to jail. He was a senator with the party in power in Illinois, and therefore he might be safe. The party would find a way to protect him and his seat, but they wouldn't be able to defend him against this gangster. Andronni's way of protection was eliminating the partners who could incriminate him.

Morrison stood with arms folded and looked out the window to the north of the city.

"This animal, Andronni bites," Morrison muttered. "I think it's time for the Marx brothers and The Evergreen Project to earn their federal and union handouts."

*   *   *

Harold Kerns was a grey-bearded man of forty-five years, large ears, and shaggy brows set over piercing eyes. He had his fingers in every illegal operation in New Orleans. He was sitting eating his Shrimp Samantha with Andouille at a Royal Street restaurant when the phone next to his glass of the Barossa-styled Shiraz vibrated.

"Yeah, Kerns here, go."

"We think the hitter has gone to Nashville. The Cincinnati police are sending the lead detective, Jake Laird, there. He'll be there to pick her up this Sunday."

"You don't want her back in Cincinnati alive, do you?"

"No, but make sure you get the package we're looking for before you do her. Call me when your people get there. I'll have all the information you'll need."

Kerns took another sip of his wine. "Who do you want me to give this to?"

"One of the Marx brothers."

"What about this cop Laird?" Kerns asked.

"They don't want him back either."

Chapter 29

"Boss, we need to talk," Phil said, walking into Commander Cohen's office. "Laird and Ferris think there's someone dirty in the department."

"Dirty? Where the hell did they get that idea?"

"Sam's partner told me when our people were in New York. They seemed to be one step behind those hit men. Laird figures someone in the department tipped them off."

"Does anyone else know about this?"

"Just us, Sam's partner Christopher, and, of course, Ferris and Laird."

"Thanks, Phil. You were right to bring this to me. Let's keep this in-house."

*   *   *

When Phil told Jake about his meeting with Cohen, it came as a shock.

"Why the hell did you tell Cohen?" Jake asked.

"Cause he's the boss. It's his division. Don't tell me you think Cohen's the mole?"

"That's not the point," Jake reminded him. "I thought since Christopher told you we were going to keep it between the four of us."

"Don't worry. It'll stay in-house. You can trust Cohen."

"Yeah, that's what they said about Benedict Arnold."

Jake didn't think Phil was the mole. He wasn't that bright, and he would have tripped himself up by now. But with Commander Ed Cohen, that's another story.

"I've looked into Lisa's jacket," Phil told Jake. "She's working girl. Don't be fooled by her age. Lisa's been a busy girl all of her life. She's a jack-of-all-trades. A stripper, a working girl, a hitter, and like most hookers she's probably into drugs. She does most of her work across the river in Covington and Newport, checks into a hotel for the day and pays up front with cash."

"I know the drill," Jake said, "I worked Vice a few years back. She probably sets up her johns by the hour and picks the hotels based on the number of tricks she has that daily."

Phil continued. "Yeah, expensive hotels if she has three or more, quick sheet joints if she's only booked one john."

Phil opened the folder on his desk and leafed through it.

"I did some checking with a friend of mine on the Newport Vice squad who knows her. He told me that she had a friend she did doubles with. He says they look like twins."

Phil looked over a sheet of paper before handing it to Jake.

"Her street name was Helen 4 You. The name on her rap sheet is Helen Kranski. She quit the business a few years back, and rumor has it she moved to Nashville."

Phil opened his desk drawer, took out a white envelope, and gave it to Jake. "Here's your plane ticket."

"You think Lisa went to her friend's place in Nashville to hide out?" Jake asked.

"If she did I don't think she went there to work the crowd at the Grand Ole Opry. They're a bit long in the tooth for her. Cohen said you should go to Nashville and check this woman out yourself."

"Cohen's is sending me to Nashville? I'm on suspension, remember? He gave you the okay to send me there?"

"The suspension will be lifted as soon as you step off the plane. Cohen thought it would be good for you to get away for a while. It might take your mind away from Sam. He wants you to be in constant communication with us while you're there."

Jake ended the conversation before Phil could start a debate about his loyalty to both him and Cohen.

Jake didn't think Cohen had a heart, but the commander was right. At the moment Jake's world revolved around catching Lisa.

Jake

Chapter 30

This was the end of a long, crazy week. Two people dead. My only good lead had come and gone when Lisa raced out the front door and into the wind.

But now it was Saturday, and since I was on a division suspension, another day off. No chasing criminals, no crime, just a day of sitting and relaxing.

Since I was involved in a shooting, Commander Cohen suspended me for three days from my regular working duties pending an in-house investigation. It would have been longer, but as it turned out, the guy I blew away was out on bail and had no business being away from New York. That made it pretty cut and dried. I tried to pull some strings to get out of counseling, but my strings weren't powerful and they broke. So eventually I'll have to sit down with the department's shrink. Hopefully, that will come much later.

If I was going to run down Lisa in Nashville tomorrow now was not the time to think about it. Today I was going to drop the curtain on Phil, Commander Cohen, this case, and veg out.

Happy days are again. It looked like Sam is finally on the mend, Veronica and I were going to visit him today, and we were finally going to spend an evening together. That was the plan. But as the Scottish poet, Robert Burns so aptly put it, "the best-laid schemes o' mice an' men often go astray." I was about to experience that first hand.

It was nine-thirty, and I was lounging on my sofa, wedging a piece of crumb cake in my mouth when the *Bee Gee's Staying Alive* went off on my phone. It couldn't be Sam. I was hoping it was Veronica, but I was disappointed on both counts. Phil sounded excited.

"Jake, did I wake you up?"

"Phil, you must be that bad feeling I woke up with this morning."

"I've got good news. You're going to feel better with me working with you in Nashville. Since Sam's going to be laid up for a while, and I'm the only other detective who's familiar with the case, Cohen assigned me to be your temporary partner."

I got up, reached over to the end table, opened a bottle of aspirins and popped a couple. I started to answer, but a gut reaction took hold of me.

Why would Cohen pair me up with Phil? What the hell was he up to? I didn't trust him. I knew I was right about keeping him out of the loop and now I have to partner with Phil?

I cut Phil off. "You're kidding me, right?"

"No, Commander Cohen wants us to work the Nashville arrest. Frankly, he thinks if we're working together you won't do your Dirty Harry impersonation again. He wants to take her alive."

"What makes him think we wouldn't just arrest her?"

"After what happened to Sam, the boss thinks you might be quick on the trigger."

I shrugged and plopped back on the sofa. Cohen might be right. It was Lisa that started us on the road to Sam getting shot. It was not my place to decide whether Cohen thought Phil could help with this investigation. I don't like it, but I work for Commander Cohen, and he decides who works the cases.

"I bet he thinks I should have fired a warning shot before I dropped the creep."

"Yeah, something like that."

"You know better than that, Phil. Nobody fires warning shots. Shooting twice is stupid. That's the crap you see on TV. It doesn't matter. We're not on the same flight, are we?"

"No, I'm driving there tomorrow morning. That way we won't have to rent a car. I'll meet you there when you step off the plane. That's when your suspension ends."

"Speaking of cars, did you check with the motor pool to see who signed out Cohen's cruiser?"

Phil said, "It wasn't me, I don't remember using it the day Sam was shot. Cullen, the motor pool boss, reminded me Commander Cohen signed for it. We talked about the upcoming season. I remember betting him the Reds would beat the Braves this season."

That's hard to believe, Phil knew jack-shit about baseball, but I had to remember who I was talking to.

"I hate to burst your bubble, Phil; the Braves look loaded. The Reds have a good team this year too."

It didn't surprise me that Commander Cohen's name was on the sign-out sheet. I didn't get a good look at the guy driving the unmarked car, but if we did have a dirty cop in the department, it looked like someone was trying to hang it around Cohen's neck.

"Jake, I'd like you to fill me in on what you know about our suspect sometime today before I go to Nashville."

"I can't. Doctor Mendenhall and I are going to try and visit Sam this afternoon. Besides, it's all in the paperwork."

"I want to know your gut feeling not what you handed in. If you're going to the hospital, Jake, make sure Christopher isn't there too. He's not your biggest fan. Cohen doesn't want to piss him off. We don't want him going to the press. Our livelihood is on the line here."

Finally an excellent piece of advice out of the mouth of Lieutenant Phil Westrope.

"Don't worry. I'll stay clear of Christopher."

Chapter 31

Later that evening, with a light rain falling, Christopher Epstein strode out of Macy's Department Store in downtown Cincinnati. He crossed Race Street and headed for the covered parking lot across from the giant retailer.

The Spring Bust-Out Dress Sale at Macy's this past week hadn't brought Christopher the figures he had last year or the crowds he had wanted.

It looks like I picked the wrong week for the sale. I hope my job isn't on the line. We only sold four-dozen pieces today, and that was for all the local stores. The sportswear buyer is having a field day. I don't know what I'm doing here. I should be at the hospital with Sam.

Christopher was lost in thought when he reached the entrance to the garage where he had parked his car.

A freckled-faced man, dressed in a Cincinnati Reds jacket, and a cigarette dangling from his mouth, exited the covered parking lot. He looked at Christopher. He let a rich smile lift the ends of his mouth and swung the door open for him.

Christopher said, "Thanks."

"No problem," the man said, switching the cigarette from his right hand to his left and sending a stream of smoke upwards.

Christopher stepped inside the first floor of the dimly lit concrete hallway and brushed the raindrops out of his hair. He pushed the up button and looked at the floor's indicator. The elevator was leaving the fourth floor, ascending to five.

"Damn it," he muttered, "It's going up. I'm parked on three. I might as well walk. I need the exercise."

He headed for the door with the red neon sign marked 'Stairs,' opened it, and took his first step to the third floor.

Christopher didn't hear the door close behind him, nor did he feel the cold metal silencer placed on the back of his head.

The suppressed pop emitted a soft echo in the stairwell. Blood trickled down from the hole in his head. He fell forward and tumbled onto the hard concrete stairs; his head twisted to the side. The gunman registered a thin smile and looked into his lifeless eyes and spoke quietly to Epstein.

"I want these guys to think I'm sloppy and at the same time send them a message," he said. He yanked the wallet out of Christopher's back pocket. He reached into his front pant pocket and pulled out a roll of bills.

"I'll leave the cash in your pockets," he said putting the rollback. "I don't want you to die broke."

The gunman bent down, picked up the spent shell casing and jammed it in his pocket. He stepped over the dead body and raced up the stairway steps two at a time. He opened the door to the second floor and looked around for his car.

A few rectangles of light coming from the overhead lights helped his eyes locate it. He reached into his jacket for his keys and unlocked the door. He removed the Cincinnati Reds jacket, rolled it into a ball, and threw it onto the back seat.

The gunman leaned over and placed his hand on the white lab coat, a clipboard, and the stethoscope that were sitting beside him on the passenger's seat.

He smiled inwardly pulled his iPhone from his pocket, and said, "Siri, take me to University hospital."

Jake

Chapter 32

Shanghai Mama's was a large open space restaurant known for its Mushroom Lollipops. They're fresh mushrooms on a stick. Veronica smiled and tugged at my coat sleeve when we entered the eatery. "How'd you know I like Chinese?"

"Your soft porcelain skin, almond eyes, and beautiful dark hair could have only come from eating Chinese food."

"I'm beginning to like you, Detective Laird. Flattery will get you everywhere."

"Laird, reservation for two," I leaned over and whispered to the brightly clad Asian woman standing at attention behind the podium.

"No need to look at a guest list, Mr. Laird. We've been expecting you. Right, this way. Your table is ready."

"Our table is ready?" Veronica said, "I didn't see you flash your badge."

"I didn't have to; the owner's a friend of mine."

We followed her toward the massive hearth at the far end of the entrance to the dining room.

Statues of Buddha and Chinese emperors gazed down at us as we marched by them single file. Paintings of red and black lacquered dragons breathing fire in our direction hung on the walls. The sharp pinging music of the Guzheng, the Chinese zither, and the four-stringed Pipa floated above us.

When we arrived at our table, she pulled Veronica's chair away and motioned her to sit.

The hostess bowed and said, "Mr. Lee asked me to make sure I call him when you arrive."

Veronica waited for the woman to walk away from the table.

"Who's this Lee fella, the owner?" Veronica asked.

"Yes."

"How do you know him?"

I told Veronica how the Cincinnati Police detained the restaurant's owner, Chang Lee, late last year when his wife, Lolita, had gone missing. Chang filed a missing person's report. A few days later he became the primary person of interest when Commander Cohen thought he did away with her.

"Did he?"

"No, Chang was cheating on his wife with one of his waitresses, so she started running around with her doctor. As it turned out, his wife and the doctor ran off to the French Riviera for a week for whatever you go to the south of France for."

"Oh, I think I remember the case," Veronica said. "Didn't you guys dig up his backyard?"

"Yeah, that pissed him off, and believe me he's not one to piss off. Chang is one tough dude. His chef told me that when he was a kid, growing up in China, it was rumored that Chang ate his moo shoo pork while the pig was still alive. When his wife got back from France, she called us and got him off the hook. Since I was the only one who thought he had nothing to do with her disappearance, we became friends. He wanted to kill her, but I kept him in check."

Veronica smiled.

"I wish we could have seen Sam," she said, changing the subject. "They were pretty strict, no visitors until tomorrow. Let's hope he's getting his strength back.

"I expected to see Christopher today," she said. "I wonder why he wasn't there."

"It's Saturday, the busiest shopping day of the week. I'm sure he'll be there tomorrow."

I turned over Veronica's wine glass without taking my eyes off her and motioned the waiter over to us.

The last time we had a drink together, she ordered a white wine. I hoped my memory had served me correctly.

"Chardonnay, right?"

She flung her black hair around, leaned toward me and looked into my eyes. "What, no champagne?"

"A Chinese restaurant is not the place to order the bubbly, but there's plenty of tea. Besides, I've got chocolate covered strawberries in the fridge and a bottle of *Taittinger* brut in a champagne bucket at my place waiting for us."

"Strawberries and Champagne." She gave me a cool smile. "You're pretty sure of yourself, aren't you, detective? You're planning on getting me to your place?"

"The possibility had crossed my mind. Champagne loses its meaning when you drink it alone."

Veronica's voice was warm and seductive. "We'll see. It all depends on how you Mirandize me."

I reached over and took her hand. "Anything you say may be used to hold you against me."

She looked at me with a spark in her eyes. "In that case, I might be tempted to make a full confession."

When the waiter arrived, I asked him, "What's the house Chardonnay?"

He laughed. "We have no fine wine or steaks, this not *Jeff Ruby's*. We have *Kendal Jackson* and *Beringer*. We also have nice Chinese rice wine, *Emperor's Own 8 and 10.*"

I looked over at Veronica who smiled and nodded her head.

"*Kendal Jackson* is fine."

"The lady will have that. I'll have a *Tsinago.*"

There was a silence for a moment. I gazed at the roaring fireplace across the room.

"You seem to be a thousand miles away," she said.

I locked my eyes on her. "I was thinking of Sam. No, that's not altogether true. I was thinking of him, but I was also thinking about us. How we've worked with one another these past few years, other than that night before you went to New York, we've never gotten together."

I leaned forward. "Are you thinking the same thing I'm thinking?"

"Yes, I wonder why the waiter didn't give us menus."

I touched her hand and smiled for a few long beats. "No, I'm serious," I said. I reached for the chopsticks and draped my black linen napkin over my lap.

"I know you are," she said placing her finger on my lips. "Unlike that night in Covington, we have the whole night ahead of us." She looked past me. "I think your owner friend is coming up the aisle."

I could see Chang's handshake coming at me.

"Jake," the short, round man called out, flashing his deep dimples. He grabbed my hand, shook it and bowed to Veronica.

"Please introduce me to lovely lady, Jake."

"Veronica Mendenhall, this is Chang Lee. Stay away from her, Chang, she's with me."

The waiter arrived with the drinks, but Chang took them from him.

"Here, Martin," Chang said, "I serve my friends. Please get our guests some of my special tea."

Chang placed the glass of wine in front of Veronica, set down the beer in front of me and bowed again.

"How are you doing, Chang?" I asked. "I haven't seen you in a while."

"I very sick man." He swung his hand around to his back. "Back bother me. Liver hurts too, but not sure where liver is, even though it bothered me. I see a doctor, but since ex-ran off with one, I don't trust doctors now."

He looked over at Veronica. "Other than that, Jake, I'm fine, thank you."

I asked Chang, "where are the menus?"

"Don't need menus."

"No Mushroom Lollipops?"

Chang looked at Veronica and smiled. "Tonight we have a special treat. Wonton stuffed with shrimp and lobster. Peking duck served with cucumber, scallions. Fresh pancakes, with special peanut sauce. For dessert, fresh coconut custard." He smiled and bowed at the waist. "I make myself."

"Thanks, Chang. I'm so hungry my stomach thinks my throat's

been cut."

Suddenly my cell vibrated.

"Excuse me," I said. I reached into my jacket pocket, removed the phone, got up, and moved a few steps away from the table.

"Jake, it's me, Phil. Where are you?"

I looked at Veronica's big blue eyes and her moist lips. She was swirling circles of the Chardonnay in her glass.

"Ascending to heaven," I told him, smiling at her. "What'd you want? It's Saturday. Phil, It's the second time you called me today. I'm on suspension, remember? I'm having dinner."

"Where?" Phil asked.

"We're at Shanghai Mama's."

"That's over on Sixth Street, right?"

"Yeah."

"Who's we?"

"Veronica Mendenhall, the medical examiner. You haven't answered me, why do you want to know where I am?"

"I'm sorry to interrupt you, but they just found Christopher Epstein lying face down in a parking lot across from Macy's with a hole in the back of his head."

"Sam's Christopher?"

"Yeah, Sam's partner. If you're on Sixth Street, you're close. Get right over there and since the M.E. is with you get her over there too. Sam would want you to be there. Don't leave until I get there."

Every fiber in my body tightened, my God, Sam's partner. I looked at Veronica and disconnected the phone. I felt like I was kicked off the suspension bridge.

"Something has happened."

"What?" she asked.

"Christopher Epstein is dead. Murdered."

"Oh my God. Where? When?"

"That was Phil. They just found him in the parking garage across from Macy's."

Veronica looked toward the front door. "That's just around the corner."

"Yeah."

"You want to go, don't you Jake?"

"I don't want to; I have to. Sam would want me there."

She nodded. "Then I'm going with you."

"You don't have to."

She riveted her tense blue eyes at me. "We're on a date, aren't we?"

"I can't believe this," I said.

Veronica shook her head "Sam is just beginning to get back to normal and then this." She cocked her head at me. "I must say, Detective Laird, you certainly are an interesting date."

Chapter 33

It was cold and raining when Veronica and I entered the dingy garage across from Macy's.

The place was crawling with cops like ants over a half-eaten cookie. Under emergency lights, and yellow crime tape, the photo unit was taking pictures of the stairway and Christopher's body.

I popped a couple of aspirins. This was one killing scene I didn't want to work. I flashed my gold badge at the tall, lanky cop standing at the entrance to the garage. He looked like he was a week out of the high school.

"Detective Laird, and this," I said pointing to Veronica, "is Doctor Mendenhall from the M.E.'s office." I raised the yellow crime scene tape, and we ducked under it.

It seemed colder as Veronica, and I put on our latex gloves. I bent down to get a better look at the hole in the back of Christopher's head.

"Who discovered the body?" I asked the officer.

"Him," he said, pointing to the guy in a University of Cincinnati jacket standing next to the vending machine.

"Since he was found on the stairs, his car couldn't have been on the first floor. It was probably on one of the upper floors. My guess is he decided to walk up. Lieutenant Westrope, from the First, is on his way. He asked me to keep you here until he arrived."

Upon examining Christopher's body, I found his wallet was

missing. When I turned him over to check his pants pockets, there was some bills in it, a set of car keys in his jacket, and a watch on his wrist.

I checked Christopher's hands and arms. "No signs of a struggle. It looks like the killer came up behind him, placed a gun to the back of his head, and pulled the trigger."

I almost couldn't believe what my eyes were telling me. This couldn't have been a robbery. There weren't any shell casings. The killer took it with him. If it were a robbery, Christopher's pockets would be empty. The killer knew exactly what he was doing. He was sending us a message.

My eyes took a frustrated 360-degree look around the stairwell. No apparent scuffle, one small caliber bullet to the back of the head. His keys were still on him, so his car was still in the garage.

A thief would have waited until he got to the victim's car before he held him up. A perp wouldn't kill him. He'd smack him around a bit, rob him, and take his car. But he certainly would have emptied all of his pockets. This was a hit.

"Here are his car keys," I said handing them to the officer. "There's a Jaguar key ring on them. There can't be too many of those up there. Start on the second floor. When you find it, place some crime scene tape around the car. Take another officer with you and have him stay with it until Lieutenant Phil Westrope gets here. I'll wait here for him and the people from forensics."

I looked around for a surveillance camera. I was disappointed, but not surprised. There wasn't one here on the first floor, but I was sure there was one at the exit booth.

"And make sure," I said, pulling him back toward me, "you get the surveillance tapes from the exit booth." I looked at my watch, "starting early this evening."

No police officer could declare Christopher Epstein legally dead, only the Medical Examiner could do that, and fortunately, she was here.

Veronica's body started to shake. I could see the sadness in her eyes.

"You okay?"

Her eyes started to tear, and she looked away. "I'm

uncomfortable."

"But you've seen this before."

Veronica's chin was quivering as she turned away from me. "I'm a doctor, a doctor who deals only in death. Never once have I even tried to save a life. Most victims I see come into the lab in body bags." She looked up the stairwell. "I guess I'm not used to seeing," she paused and looked back at the body, "a victim who is connected to the department. I don't understand it. Why would anyone kill a man just to take his wallet?"

"This was a hit, made to look like a robbery gone bad. A real thief would have taken all of his money, and his car. When do you figure it happened?"

She took a deep breath. "Body's still warm." Veronica ran her fingers over the blood on Christopher's neck.

"The blood is just beginning to clot. I'd say less than an hour ago."

Veronica reminded me, "It takes about fifteen minutes for blood to coagulate. Everyone is different depending on the medication they're taking and their age. I'd say, in the absence of any medication he may have been taking, he was shot around the time we were going into the restaurant."

She rose to her feet and snapped off her latex gloves.

"By the look of the wound, I say the killer was shorter than Christopher."

"How's that?" Veronica asked.

"He's lying here on the first four steps. The wound looks like the gun was pointing up."

"A better look at the lab will give us that answer," Veronica pointed out.

I said, "Anyone using the elevator wouldn't have seen the body. That guy over there, in the UC jacket, must have been the first to use the stairway after the killing."

"Why Christopher?"

"How the hell would I know?" I lied. I warned Phil about it, but he wouldn't listen. I pulled Veronica aside, scratched my head and pointed to Christopher's body.

"Something's strange," I told her. "When Phil called, he knew who the victim was. How? The killer took Christopher's wallet."

I started toward the guy who'd discovered the body when Lieutenant Phil Westrope swung open the door and walked through.

I was sneaking up on the killer's motive. Then it hit me, the mole. Sam sealed Christopher's fate by telling him our theory that someone in the department was working against us, and he told Phil. Phil told Cohen. It had to be one of them. If the killer was eliminating the people who knew about the mole in the department, Sam could be next. And my ass was on the line too.

I managed a weak smile. "I'm glad you're finally here, lieutenant," I said. "I didn't see anyone standing guard outside of Sam's room this afternoon. Commander Cohen didn't sign the order?"

Phil took a drag on his cigarette and shook his head no.

"He wasn't allowed visitors, why have a guard? He left yesterday for a conference in Columbus before I could get him to sign the paperwork."

I stood there ratcheting my mind the possible reasons for Phil not getting the okay from Cohen before he left.

"Why didn't you sign the order?"

"I didn't have the time. I'll sign the report when I get back to the squad room."

I swallowed my disappointment.

Phil removed a pack of cigarettes from his pocket, shook one out and lit it from the one he was already smoking.

I asked Phil, "How did you know it was Sam's partner lying in the stairway? The killer took his wallet."

"You didn't do a very good job interrogating the officer who called this in, did you? The guy who found him worked at Macy's. He identified the victim as Christopher Epstein because he knew him."

I sucked in my breath, trying to keep quiet, then pushed past him.

"Where the hell you going?" he asked.

"To be with Sam. There's a mole in the division, remember?" It came out of my mouth so unexpectedly it hadn't dawned on me what I had just suggested.

Phil shook his head. "Stay away from there. Besides, you can't go until you're finished here."

"I'm on suspension until we get off the plane in Nashville."

"Yeah, and that means stay the hell away from the hospital."

A fire was building up inside me. "Bullshit, I'm going to be with my partner."

I looked at Phil, saw anger flash in his face. "Damn it, Jake there are no visiting hours for Sam."

I wanted to high five his face but didn't have the time to get into a battle with him. I looked at Phil and pointed to Christopher's dead body.

"Sam could be next. I don't want to see my partner lying in a hospital with a bullet hole in his head. You better get on the horn, lieutenant, and have a squad car get over to University to guard him. His next visitor might not give a shit about whether there's visiting hours or not."

* * *

"Is that you, boss?" Phil asked, answering his cell.

"Yes, Phil, it's me," answered Commander Cohen. "My secretary just called and said there was a shooting downtown."

"Yes, there was. It was in the public parking garage across from Macy's. That makes seven in downtown garages this year, and it's only the middle of April. You're not going to believe this. The victim was identified as Christopher Epstein, Sam Ferris's partner. Remember, he's the guy who told me about the mole in our department. Laird thinks it looks like a hit."

"A hit? No, I doubt it. It was probably a terrible coincidence. This guy was in the wrong place at the wrong time."

"But this guy Epstein knew about the mole theory Laird, and Ferris have," Phil said. "If it was a hit, Laird thinks Ferris could be next. I'm sending a couple of men to University Hospital to stand watch.

"Why, lieutenant?" Cohen asked. "They have their own security. Call them and get some of their men on it. Think of what the press will do if they find out we used police officers to guard one of our own. How would it look to you if we needed policemen to guard a policeman?"

"It's too late, sir," Phil said. "I assigned a man to guard outside Detective Ferris's room."

"Get them the hell out of there, and do it now."

Cohen put his hand over the receiver, and announced angrily, "Phil, I have to go. I hate to interrupt you, but the phone in my room is ringing; it's probably my wife. I promised I'd call her before she turned in. Phil, tell the press it was a robbery. We don't want them reporting we have a killer on the loose. And Phil," Cohen demanded, "get those men away from Detective Ferris's room and back on the street."

Chapter 34

Driving back to the hospital, Veronica asked me what I thought of Phil.

"Every now and then I have to contradict myself and believe that maybe Phil isn't as dumb as he appears. Then I realize Commander Cohen was smart to hide Phil behind a desk. He's dangerous no matter whether he has a pen or a gun in his hands."

Veronica nodded. "You got that right. I don't think his elevator goes all the way to the top. In fact, the first time I met him he asked me how many autopsies I had performed on dead people that day."

"What'd you tell him?"

"All of them. The live ones put up too much of a fight."

*   *   *

University Hospital was a fifteen-minute drive from downtown Cincinnati. We parked by the Emergency entrance, flashed our badges at the nurse on duty, and headed for the elevators. I punched the button for the seventh floor.

When we exited the elevator, Veronica, smiled at the rosy-cheeked nurse sitting behind her desk. She was staring at the little strips of light that danced across the cardiac monitors. She recognized us from earlier in the day.

"Hello again," Veronica said waving at her. "I see you're still on duty."

"The nurse looked over her shoulder, tapped her fingers on the desk, and pointed to the clock on the wall. "My relief is late again."

I spoke up, "My boss is sending a police officer over to guard Detective Ferris. Has he arrived yet?"

"No one's checked in."

"How's he's doing?"

"He's out of the coma and resting comfortably. What he needs now are peace and quiet. Please keep your people outside of his room."

I looked at Veronica. "Thank God."

We started down the hall to Sam's room as two guys from the precinct stepped off the elevator. Charlie's wavy hair stuck out from under the Cincinnati Reds cap. Although Charlie was only a little over five-seven, he walked off the elevator as though he owned the place.

"It's Saturday. No date tonight, Charlie?"

"I broke up with my girl a couple of weeks ago. Lieutenant Westrope called and said Commander Cohen didn't want cops guarding cops, so I was pulled off." He registered a weak smile.

"Since I had nothing to do tonight I figured I'd do it on my own time. Sam's my racquetball partner on the division's racquetball team. I told the lieutenant I'd stand guard as a private citizen."

Charlie's smile disappeared as he looked down the hall. "Is he still in a coma?"

"No, but the nurse wants you to stay out of his room."

"Does he know about Christopher?"

"No, I'll tell him when I feel the time is right. I don't want him to hear it from anyone but me."

"What room is he in?"

"702. I appreciate you coming," I said. "I'll be back around three or four at the latest. And you, Tom?" I asked the officer standing next to Charlie.

Tom shrugged and cast a sheepish glance at Charlie. He removed a plastic bottle of water from his pocket and took a swig.

"You know, without his main squeeze, Charlie needs someone

to keep him company."

Veronica wrapped her arm around my shoulder. "I know you're concerned about Sam, but now that he's out of the coma, and the nurse said not to go into his room, we might as well continue our date."

"I just want to make sure he's being covered by one of our own."

"You promised me an unusual dinner, and I'm famished."

I slipped my arm around Veronica's waist and drew her close.

"Most restaurants have stopped serving by now, but I did promise you a dinner. Jake Laird always delivers on his promises." I took my phone from my pocket and ran my fingers over the keypad.

"You want sausage or pepperoni on your pizza?"

"Champagne goes with everything. Make mine a veggie."

*   *   *

We left the hospital and drove back through the tree-lined streets of Glendale. The pizza was ordered, half sausage, half veggie and we were finally alone and in my apartment.

"Where's your dog, Maggie?" Veronica asked.

"At the vets. I'm going to Nashville tomorrow. I sent her to the shelter."

"The shelter?"

"The place I rescued her."

"I didn't know you rescued her from a shelter."

"It's not really a shelter. It's a place called The Orphans of The Storm."

I took her jacket and pointed her to the kitchen.

Veronica started to open the kitchen cabinet doors. "Where do you hide your dishes? I want to set the table."

"I usually eat my pizza right out of the box."

"You're on a date. Open the champagne, and we'll have a glass while we're waiting for the pizza."

Veronica opened the refrigerator, placed the chocolate covered strawberries on the top rack, and gasped. "There's nothing in here!"

I kicked off my Bass Weejuns. "I beg your pardon, there's a six pack of Bud, half dozen eggs, a jar of pickles, and a box of baking soda in there. What else does a bachelor need?"

"Jake," Veronica said, closing the door, "I'll tell you one thing you don't need. It's the baking soda."

"But there is a need for this," I said, taking the *Taittinger* Brut from the bucket. I wrapped a towel around the top of the bottle and popped the cork.

Veronica found the long stemmed champagne glasses in the kitchen cabinet, put them on the cocktail table, and filled them with bubbly.

I sat back, buried myself deep in the cushions of my brown leather sofa, and looked across at Veronica. She held out her hand. I squeezed it gently and pulled her next to me.

"Let's have a toast to Sam's quick recovery and resolve to avenge Christopher's killing. I've waited a long time for us to be together like this."

She took my hand and ran it along her cheek and kissed my fingers. She turned my hand over pressing her lips to my palm.

Our eyes locked. We leaned toward each other, her soft, warm red lips slightly touching mine. Our legs moved against one another's beneath the cocktail table. She slipped off her shoes, reached under her sweater and unhooked her bra.

The ringing at the front door interrupted the moment.

"Damn it, terrible timing," I said. "Must be the pizza."

She widened her blue eyes and whispered. "Get the door. I promise you we'll pick up where we left off."

*   *   *

The late April moon that shone through the window bathing the bed with a pale white glow spread throughout the bedroom. I smiled as the memories of the night flashed through my mind. The sex was so good I bet my next door neighbor had a cigarette.

I went into the bathroom, looked in the mirror, and ran my hand over the stubble of my beard.

"I looked at my watch. It was 5:30 in the morning. I had to get back to the hospital. I'll shave later."

I came out of the bathroom, pulled on my jeans and buttoned my shirt. I gazed down at Veronica, still sleeping peacefully with a broad smile on her face. I felt a little awkward. I wanted to reach down to wake her but thought better of it.

I made my way into the living room where I thought I'd leave her a note. I found a piece of paper, scribbled a quick on it, and propped it against the empty champagne bottle.

Hi,

Call me on my cell when you wake. Keep yourself and the pizza warm. I'd like to have both of you for breakfast.

Jake

Chapter 35

Phil was a little late, so it was almost 8:30 when I left the hospital. Veronica buzzed me and said she had gotten a call from the M.E.'s office. The weekend-shift M.E. called in sick. The stiffs weren't going anywhere, but she had to cover for him anyway. Veronica told me not to worry and that she'd call a cab to take her home.

Sunday afternoon, April 22 was a dazzler of a day in Cincinnati. Not a cloud in the sky, just a hint of a breeze blowing across the Ohio River, a great day to fly.

My Mustang started to misfire on the way to the airport. I wanted the problem to be fixed before I got back from Nashville. I drove to the motor pool on Ezzard Charles Drive and picked up an unmarked.

When I arrived at the garage, Sergeant Pat Cullen, the officer who runs the department's motor pool, was stuffing French fries in his mouth. He finished the last of his Big Mac, crushed the McDonald's wrapper, and tossed it in the trash.

Three years ago Pat was shot when he walked in on a gas station stick-up in Avondale. His left shoulder was so severely damaged he lost partial use of his arm. Naturally, this kept him off street duty. Pat was a certified Ford mechanic when he entered the police academy. He was offered a desk job, or he could file for disability. He declined both because he wanted to pull his own weight. Pat asked to be assigned to the motor pool. It was a perfect fit for the division and for him.

I could smell the oil and gasoline fumes as I stepped over the grease and water on the floor. A line of cruisers and un-marks waited in various stages of repair.

Pat stuffed the rest of the fries in his mouth and brushed the salt off his fingertips. He held out his hand. "Hey, Jake."

"No thanks, Pat," I said moving my hand away, "I'm on a salt-free diet."

We walked into his office, and I closed the door behind me. Pat, rubbed his hands together, sat down, and laughed. "Sorry, what can I do for you?"

"My ride is acting up again, and I need a ride to go to the airport."

"No problem. What do you want?"

"Charger, a Crown Vic, I don't care as long as it makes it across the river."

"How's Sam?"

"Not so good, but he's out of the coma. When you get a chance look in on him."

Pat leaned forward in his chair. His face broadened with a sheepish grin. "I wanted to see him last Tuesday. I called his room number, but they told me he couldn't have any visitors. The Cardinals were in town, and I didn't want the tickets I had to go to waste."

I gave him a strange look.

"What?" He asked, cocking his head.

"You're a Braves fan. Why the hell would you spend money to see the Cardinals?"

Pat looked at me blankly. "I'm from St. Louis, remember? Who told you I was a Braves fan?"

That remark stunned me. I got that bullshit story from Phil. "Phil Westrope."

I should have braced myself for what was coming. Pat leaned forward, raising his voice. "Don't get me started. That weasel?

What the hell does he know? He's Commander Cohen's flunky. He's got his head up the boss's ass," he said pointing across the room. "If he weren't related to Cohen's wife he'd be mopping those toilets,"

"Phil told me he came in here last week and made a bet with you that the Reds would have a winning record against the Braves."

I pulled out my notepad. I flipped the pages looking for the plate number of the unmarked I followed from the airport.

"Who gives a shit about the Braves. Atlanta is in the eastern division. The Cards and the Reds are in the Central. You're pretty dense," Pat said. "Write this down in that notebook you're holding: I'm a Cardinal fan."

"Yeah, it was Phil. Tell me, who checked out the unmarked with plate number 76HAM77?"

"That's Cohen's Dodge Charger."

Pat punched a few buttons on the keyboard, and then he paused to look at the monitor. "Westrope came in here yesterday and signed it out for a trip to Nashville."

"Who signed it out last week?"

"What day?"

Pat turned the monitor toward me.

"The day Sam was shot, the tenth."

He danced the cursor up and down the screen.

Pat's mouth moved, but nothing came out. Finally, he said, turning the screen toward me, "that's Commander Cohen's name on the sign-out sheet. We need a physical signature. After he signed the book, we transposed the information from the book to the computer."

Pat walked to the other side of his office. I stood behind him and looked over his shoulder.

He opened a desk drawer and took out a book labeled 'Cincinnati Vehicle Register.'

"April tenth?"

"Yeah."

He sat for a couple of seconds turning the pages of the register.

"That's funny. It says Cohen signed it out."

"Why is it so funny?"

"Cohen hasn't used the department's vehicle since his kid dropped out of Ohio State."

"What does he use?"

"His personal vehicle."

"Cohen's convertible?"

Pat's eyes widened as if he had just remembered something. "Yeah, the Corvette. He didn't want his kid near it."

"And you didn't see Phil last Saturday."

"That's the day Sam got shot, right? The tenth?"

"Yeah."

"No, yesterday was the first time I've seen Phil in a month."

Pat closed the register and started to walk back to his desk.

I sprang on him. "How can you be so sure? You didn't look."

He looked over his shoulder at me.

"I'm in the same union you're in," he replied. "We get our birthdays off, remember? That's the day I turned fifty. Beltera opened the weekend before, and my wife and I went to the track. Then we went down and watched my Cardinals kick the shit out of the Reds."

Pat went back to his desk, sat and turned his computer monitor toward me. The month of April was still up, and he placed the curser alongside April 10th. He then pointed to the screen. "It must have been Lopez who signed him in."

I was feeling numb all over. It was Phil Westrope who picked up the two hit men at the airport. He had to be the mole.

"Is Lopez here?" I asked.

Pat shook his head. "No, he doesn't work on Sundays. It looks like Cohen signed out for his car that day."

"Take a look at my Mustang, will ya? I said. "The valves sound like they're sticking and the transmission's acting up."

"I thought you had a guy in Wyoming work on your car."

"Yeah, but he charges me."

"Your friend is still the traveling secretary of the Reds, right?"

I knew where this was going.

"Yeah."

"My wife and I are going to St. Louis to visit her mom on Memorial Day. The Phillies will be in town. Get me a couple of club seats and your ride will run like new."

"Deal."

Pat got up, took a set of keys from the board, and tossed them to me. He handed me the book to sign and pointed across the garage toward a black Ford Vic.

"Sign here and bring it back in one piece."

I signed the register and gave him a thumbs-up.

I turned to leave, but Pat wasn't finished.

"Take a tip from an old friend," he said. "Don't wrestle in the mud with that pig Westrope. You'll both get dirty, but likes it."

Lisa

Chapter 36

I knew the Cincinnati Police had pictures of me, and information about my car was guaranteed to be on all point bulletins. Thank God I had a change of clothes in the trunk. It's a good thing I pulled into a rest area and got rid of the robe. Now, the question is where am I going to hide? My friend Helen, who worked with me in Atlantic City, lives just outside Nashville. She'd put me up for a few days. I'll spend some time with her and share a few beers and maybe poke my head out for the mandatory trip to Opryland.

Carmine's connection to the mob taught me to prepare for emergencies. I can hear the bastard now:

"When you're on the run, whether from the law or from your own crew, always keep an overnight bag and a license plate from another state in the trunk of your car. Make sure you have a few changes of clothes and a fake driver's license. Never use a credit card. Disassemble and ditch your cell phone. Keep some cash, wrapped in tin foil, in a bag. At least a thousand dollars made up of the twenties, fifties, and a few Ben Franklins and most important, have a piece with plenty of ammunition. And never, but never, go over the speed limit or bring attention to yourself."

After I changed into my clothes, I still had two problems. First, I was about out of cash, but the amount I had in the trunk was nowhere near what I was going to need. I didn't dare use a credit card. The other problem was the piece. I shouldn't have thrown the damn thing at the cop who ran in on my firefight with Andronni's man.

My eyes flickered back and forth between the rear view mirror and the road ahead. A black sedan, flashing red and blue, came up behind me. Just my luck, an unmarked highway patrol car.

I looked at the dashboard. I wasn't going over the speed limit. Maybe he wasn't pulling me over.

I slumped, turned my head away, and looked over my right shoulder. I breathed a sigh of relief as the black vehicle flashed by me. He's probably going for his afternoon fix of *Dunkin Donuts*.

I drove slowly so as not to draw attention. Although the trip to Nashville was a five-hour ride at this speed, I needed the time and gathered my thoughts about Andronni's people.

From what I saw on the flash drive about Senator Morrison, my guess is a hit man, from Illinois, has a contract out on me.

There were a lot of questions I needed to be answered before I dropped in on Helen.

The last time we spoke, she was still living with a truck driver who moved in with her. Was he on the road? Her kids walked out a couple of years ago. Was she alone?

A thought flashed through my mind. I signaled and pulled onto the shoulder of the interstate.

My dilemma began to sink in slowly. Andronni's men found me by beating the information out of Eddie. The Cincinnati police had my phone records. I called Helen a few weeks ago. With her number taken from my call list, the police had to have her address. Nashville was suddenly out. Going there was too dangerous.

Sweat trickled down between my breasts. I began to feel the air squeezing in on me. I needed a drink. I reached over, opened the glove compartment, and pulled out the bottle of Johnnie Walker Red.

Then it hit me how stupid that would be. After everything else that had happened, what brand of idiot would get pulled over with whiskey on their breath?

The blood began to pound in my temple. I didn't parachute in here yesterday. I've got to get myself together.

That cheap bastard Andronni, he paid me ten grand to put Hank to sleep. Five grand up front. Then puts a contract out on me so he can save the other five thousand.

Screw the Dago bastard. I have an ace in the hole, the flash drive. It's about time I stuck it up his ass.

Jake

Chapter 37

When you've been a detective as long as I have, you grow a sharp nose for where a case is going. Traveling to Nashville to arrest Lisa didn't feel right. Although I felt a developing situation there, my thoughts still bounced around like I was dodging potholes on I-75.

Commander Cohen determined Lisa was on her way to Music City. He had Phil call the Kentucky and Tennessee State Police with the description of the car registered to Lisa Turnbull. He gave the Nashville police the address of her friend, Helen Kranski so they could stake out the home. If she were dumb enough to show up, she'd be taken in. That would be the end of this case. So why the hell would Cohen send me there? And why was I going with Phil? Why did Phil choose to drive to Nashville?

It was 1:30 that afternoon before I arrived at the airport. I drove to Delta's terminal parking area. I got out of my car and waited for the shuttle bus to the airport.

When the bus arrived, I found a seat behind the bus driver. I was about to open the new bestseller, *Seeds of the Lemon Grove*, when my cell went off. I fumbled for it in my jacket pocket and looked at the number. Eight fifty-nine, the Northern Kentucky area code.

"Jake Laird."

The voice came out in a whisper. "Hey, sweetheart, this is Lisa Turnbull."

The hairs on my arm stood up, and my mind began to race. I stood up quickly and nudged my way past the other passengers toward the back of the bus.

"I was wondering when you'd get around to calling me. Where'd you get my number?"

"Never mind where I got it. I got it."

"Aren't you supposed to be on your way to Nashville?"

"Do you really think I'm that stupid to go where my phone records pointed you?"

"The thought entered my mind."

"Where are you now?" she asked.

"I'm at the airport."

I had no idea what was coming my way. Her voice came back in a dictatorial tone.

"Go back to your car, get on 75, and drive toward Lexington."

"You want to turn yourself in?"

"For killing that bastard? Now there's an ugly thought. Those mafia goons were sent to hit me. One of them was shooting at both of us. It was self-defense."

"What about Thompson? That didn't look like self-defense to me."

"Look, Laird, I'd like to have this tete-a-tete with you, but we don't have a lot of time. I've got something people who want to get their hands on."

"The flash drive?"

"Bingo. I'm in a hailstorm. I can't run, I can't hide, and I can't make it stop. I've got the New York mob and an Illinois congressman, and you chasing my ass. Someone is eventually going to catch me, and sweetheart, as crazy as it sounds, I want it to be you."

"Why?"

"The minute those bastards catch me, I'm toast. You, on the other hand, will put me on trial, put me in jail, and then maybe in twenty years, you'll toast me."

"Why don't you just give it to them?"

"Boy, you guys don't get it. If I give it to them, I'll wind up floating down the Ohio River. If I don't, they'll beat it out of me like they did Eddie."

"Then turn yourself in and give it to me."

"No thanks."

"It looks like you don't have a whole lot of options, sweetheart. I'm the only friend you have. If you turn yourself in, and there's something on that flash drive we can use, I might be able to get the prosecutor to drop the charge to involuntary manslaughter."

"I don't think so, sweetie. I intended to kill the bastard. It was a hit."

"We know that. It will be better for you, Lisa, if you turn yourself over to me."

"We'll talk about that when you get here."

"You better stay where you are. Don't go near Nashville. They have no intention of taking you alive. They want the flash drive."

"Why would the Cincinnati police want me dead?"

"I think the guy, waiting for you in Nashville, is a dirty cop, and he's taking his orders from Andronni. Stay away and tell your friend to get the hell out of her house."

"Okay, then I want you to meet me here," she said.

"Where's here?"

"Do you know where the Toyota plant is off of I-75?"

"Just north of the Georgetown exit, right?"

"Yeah. If you leave now, it should take you about an hour to get here."

"Then what?" I asked.

"Then I'll call you again. And don't try to have this number checked."

"It's a throwaway, isn't it?"

"Right again. Jake, you're not only pretty, but you're also bright."

"You're a funny girl. But my boss isn't laughing, Lisa. Why am I driving to Lexington if you're not going to turn yourself in?"

"I need to trust someone, and it's beginning to look like you."

"Trust me? But why should I trust you? The last time you and I were together, we were in the middle of that firefight, you ran out on me."

"You were great, and I hear you killed the bastard. It says in your jacket you graduated from the University of Dayton Law School."

"How'd you know that?"

"Never mind," she said, "Do you still have a license to practice law in Ohio?"

I sat paralyzed while wondering how to answer. "Yeah, Why? I renew it yearly."

"I have a proposition for you and I believe it's time for us to meet.

Jake

Chapter 38

The shuttle bus started to fill up for the trip to Delta's terminal.

The driver kept his eyes on the people exiting the shuttle who were going into the terminal.

When the shuttle emptied, the driver looked over his shoulder and barked at me. "Hey, mister, this is the last stop. You getting off?"

I felt oddly embarrassed. "I'm sorry," I said. "I need to get back to my car."

Too many unanswered questions. Why did Lisa want to meet if she wasn't turning herself in or giving me the flash drive?

When I got off the bus, my cell went off.

"Jake, it's Cullen. That bullshit about Phil telling you I was a Braves fan bothered me. Since Lopez was on duty that day, I called him. He doesn't understand why Cohen's name is on the registry. Phil signed Cohen's Charger out."

I let out a slow breath. "Lopez sure it was the same day?"

"Yeah, Lopez said Sam brought his cruiser in to change a tire. Phil signed Cohen's Charger couple of hours earlier. Phil returned the car just after Sam left. That's when Lopez heard that Sam had been shot. That's hard to forget."

It flashed in my mind so quickly that it didn't dawn on me what

Cullen had just said. The mole had to be Phil.

"Thanks for the information, Pat."

Cullen's statement felt like an elbow to my gut. I shook my head in disbelief. I scrolled my thoughts back over the last few days for any details that might have pointed to Phil. While we were giving him our progress on finding Lisa, Phil was passing that information along to his handlers in New York.

When I got to my car, my phone went off again. I knew this was coming; it was Phil.

"Detective Laird."

"Where are you, Jake?"

"En route to Nashville. I missed the plane, Phil."

"What the hell were you doing? Screwing around with that M.E? Damn it, Jake, I need you here."

"For Christ's sake, Phil, I told you I'm on my way."

"Where'd you say you were?"

"I'm fifty miles south of Louisville and should be in Nashville in a couple of hours." I looked at the clock on the dashboard, "Around five."

"Hurry, you're screwing up all my arrangements," Phil said. "I don't want to take her without you."

"I'll meet you at the hotel."

"No, come right to Lisa's friend's house. I've asked the locals to hang back and let us do our thing. You do have the address I gave you?"

"Yeah, I have it."

I don't understand Phil's reasoning. Why have the local cops hang back? Why not just have them arrest Lisa. Now that I know he's the mole, I have to wonder what he's up to.

"Okay, Phil, I'll see you around five. Bye."

Should I call Cohen and have Phil taken into custody and brought him back to Cincinnati? Probably, but first, now that Lisa was in the wind, I needed to find out what was up her sleeve.

Chapter 39

Phil Westrope stood at the Delta gate in Nashville waiting for Flight 434 to empty. He couldn't get Jake out of his mind. Why did Jake miss the flight? What was he up to?

Phil forced a smiled looking at the guy with the red hair, exiting the ramp, walking toward him. The guy was dirty. Even the whites of his eyes looked soiled.

Phil moved his eyes to the man's forehead, his chin, his left ear, and then his right ear, the sign of the cross. In the police academy, it was the procedure the recruits were taught to size up a witness.

"How was your flight?" Phil asked.

Red Marx was trim, well built, around five-seven, and wore a red golf shirt over a pair of well-worn jeans.

"It was okay. When's your guy coming in?"

Phil shook his head. "He's not."

"How come?"

"I don't know, and I don't like it, but I'm glad to meet one of the other Marx brothers finally."

"The pleasure is all yours," Marx answered. "You know my brothers?"

"I was in Delpinto's crew with your brother Bob before you guys went independent," Phil said. "There were two things I remember about him. One thing the crew said was he didn't worship the devil the devil worshipped him. We called him Groucho because of his shitty mustache."

"Well, he shaved it off," Marx said; "now they call him The Ghost."

"The Ghost?"

"You don't see him coming, and when he's done, you don't see him leave. And I don't have his fucking sense of humor, so don't call me Harpo." Marx looked around again. "Why isn't your guy coming?"

"He said he missed his flight."

"That saved his life, at least for now."

"Got any bags?"

"No, just this," he pointed to the ratty-looking brown knapsack hanging over his shoulder. "And the shit in the package I sent you. Where is it?"

"It's in the trunk of my car," Phil answered. "What's in it?"

"Never mind I'll tell you when we get there. You have plenty of ammo, right? Look, I'm sure your people told you this is my show," Marx reminded Phil. "If anything goes wrong I'm the one who'll get whacked."

Phil nodded.

"You didn't answer me. You got enough ammo?"

"More than we'll need for this job."

"You got the locals covered?"

"I called the Nashville police and gave them the address of an apartment complex on the other side of town where we think this broad's holed up," Phil said smiling. "They wanted to go in without me, but I asked them to create a perimeter around the complex and wait until I got there. That way we could go in together."

"Won't that get your ass in trouble when they find you gave them the wrong address?"

Phil smiled again as if acknowledging the problem. "Since we're not taking the broad alive, and we're going to blow Jake's head off in the firefight, that will be the end of the case."

They exited the terminal and headed for the parking garage as it was beginning to rain.

Phil said, "I'm worried about Jake not being here. I know

there's got to be a reason he didn't get on the plane. It wasn't car trouble. I don't think he ever intended to come here. Something's changed."

Marx had a satisfied smirk on his face

"Don't worry about your detective friend. Since he's not here, he won't be in our way. Let's get what we came for and then do the bitch."

"Nice job with the queer in the parking building, but how'd you miss the cop in the hospital? The people in Chicago are pissed."

"My brothers and I work like hell for them all the time. But those guys in Chicago don't know how to be grateful. I too got an earful this morning, but they don't understand. I couldn't whack the guy with the guard in the room."

"I figured that was the reason, but I wasn't sure. I pulled that cop off duty," Phil said, "but he volunteered to do it on his own time." Phil shook his head. "I'm still wondering why Jake didn't get on that plane."

Max said, "Not to worry. My brother is meeting me in Cincy after he whacks Thompson's wife in Chicago."

"You're not doing her together?"

"No, he has his job, and I have mine."

"No loose ends, huh?"

"She may know more than she's supposed to," Max replied. "New York doesn't like loose ends. One of us will kill the guy in the hospital."

When they got to the Charger, Phil unlocked the door. Marx pulled a pint of Jack Daniels from his knapsack. He drained the bottle, threw it under the car next to Phil's cruiser. The glass danced in all directions. Then he wiped his mouth with the back of his bony hand. He stepped into the car, looked over at Phil with a twisted grin, and closed the door.

"Come on my friend; let's go kill some people."

Jake

Chapter 40

I walked down the main terminal weaving my way through the group of teenagers on their cell in front of the Delta gate marked 'Spring Break.' It was a chartered flight going to Daytona Beach. Stopping at Starbucks, I bought myself a cup of overpriced black coffee.

My phone rang. "Detective Laird, Commander Cohen, here. Let me talk to Westrope. I can't get him on his phone."

"He's not with me, sir," I said. "He drove to Nashville."

"Drove? Is he not with you? I thought you guys were going together so you could bring him up-to-date on the case."

"It was his idea to drive, sir. He wanted me to fly. My car was giving me trouble, so I picked up an unmarked at the motor pool. That delay caused me to miss my flight. I'm going to drive back to Cincinnati."

Cohen said, "Try to get Phil on the horn. Tell him you're driving to Nashville."

"He can carry on without me, sir. It'll take five hours to get there. They don't need me. Between the local people and the lieutenant, they should be able to bring Lisa in. I still have a lot of paperwork."

"Forget the paperwork for now," Cohen said. "You'll have plenty of time for that when you get back to town."

I paused, thinking about what to say next, and ran my fingernails over the phone speaker. "We're breaking up, sir. I'm having trouble hearing you."

"I said put the paperwork aside for now. Go to Nashville. Phil insisted you be there."

Good. I can get lost for a few hours. Phil will think I'm on my way to meet him, but it will be Lisa I'll be meeting. The last thing I need is to let Phil know Lisa is going to be a no-show.

"There's something wrong with this phone, sir. I'm having trouble hearing you.... you're breaking up."

I sucked my breath in. I could hear Cohen yelling, "Jake, I can't hear you, what was that?"

I snapped the cell shut. Oh my God, what a day, just what I need the boss looking over my shoulder.

First I was going to Nashville, then one phone call, and I wasn't. I was going there to arrest Lisa, and now I'm going to meet her in Georgetown. I had to keep this line open for her call. I needed time to make some sense of what she was up to. Was she playing me? It wasn't a good idea to keep a woman waiting, especially a cold-blooded killer.

Chapter 41

Dark clouds began to settle over Nashville, threatening a spring storm. Phil guided the Dodge Charger off Briley Parkway onto Interstate 40 for the ride to downtown Nashville.

Red Marx looked over at Phil. "This detective guy, Jake, he's a friend of yours?"

"He's been a thorn in my side ever since I joined the department." Phil gave Marx an inadvertent smile. "He's no friend. He's just a cop who's outlived his usefulness. He may be getting close to figuring out who's tipping off our friends in New York."

"Tell me," Marx asked, "if this broad had a contract to hit New York's money guy, why are they after her? She did her job."

Phil shrugged. "She was supposed to upload the mark's information into a flash drive and send it to the people in New York."

"And she didn't?"

"No, they think she's going to blackmail our friend in New York," Phil replied. "I'm afraid she's given you independents a bad name. You know those guys in the Andronni family. You have to follow their instructions, or you wind up in the river decked out in grey cement shoes and a chain necklace. You can't trust you, independents."

Max gave Phil a fixed stare. "What the hell do you mean by that?"

"I mean exactly that," Phil said, offering a tired smile. "I know it's counterintuitive, but it's true. Keeping it in-house made more sense."

"Well, I understand they sent two of your houseboys after her, and they're both lying on a table in the morgue." Rubbing the back of his neck, Marx continued. "They finally gave us the job. It will be a pleasure to show those guys in New York they should have called the Marx brothers first."

Just as they pulled off Interstate 10, the sky opened.

"Rain is the last thing I need right now. Where's this woman live?" Marx asked.

"We caught a break," Phil said, downshifting as they went into a tight right-hand curve. "She lives in Salemtown; it's a run-down neighborhood."

"So?"

Phil's smile disappeared. "You know how they are. There are always killings in these run-down sections of town. Nobody will give a shit."

"Where's the fire department?" Marx asked.

Phil stared at Marx, his eyes shifted suspiciously. "I have no idea. They probably don't have one. Why?"

"Get on the horn and check where the closest one is."

Phil cocked his head, tapped his fingers on the steering wheel and stared at Marx. "I don't like the sound of that. Where's the fire?"

Marx shrugged; he looked bored. "In the trunk of this car."

Chapter 42

Helen Kranski sat at her kitchen table in the north section of downtown Nashville. Her live-in, Carl Gomes, all 260 pounds of him, sat across from her eating a grilled cheese sandwich and gulping down a can of Budweiser.

"You better close those windows, babe," Carl's voice boomed. "It's getting dark. Looks like we're in for a hell of a storm."

"It's starting to rain now, babe," she said. "When's your Dallas run start?"

"I got about an hour before I need to check in with the dispatcher," Carl said looking at his watch. "I'll wait until it lets up before I go in. The weather report said showers were moving through late this afternoon. It looks like those weather guys are going to be right for a change. When's your friend from Cincinnati getting here?"

"I forgot to tell you," Helen said. "Lisa called this morning. She's had a change in plans. She's not coming."

"That's too bad," Gomes, said, "it would have been nice to have an old friend keep you company while I made my run to Texas."

*   *   *

Phil guided the Charger past a row of rundown duplexes in The Maple Crest housing project. The farther they got from the interstate, the poorer the neighborhood became.

Most of the windows on the houses were covered with plywood

or plastic. The street was littered with beer cans and bottles that made it look like the Rolling Stones had just finished a concert.

At the end of the road, next door to Helen Kranski's house was a rundown warehouse. Her place stood by itself on a small lot surrounded by a splintered, grey, picket fence. Between the warehouse and Helen's house were bushes and a four-foot chain link fence. Phil parked the Charger across from the warehouse.

"Hot dog, an empty building," Marx said, pointing to the red, abandoned, brick structure. "I can use that place as a cover before I blow the fucking house up."

Marx looked like he was enjoying himself. Phil's eyes drifted toward Helen's faded, clapboard house.

"Blow it up?" Phil asked. "What the hell you have in my trunk, a bomb?"

"Yeah, something like that."

Marx got out of the car. His eyes drifted again to the dilapidated shell of the warehouse. "Get me the package I sent you and then stay in the car. Oh, where's the nine I asked you to get?"

"It's in the package."

"Watch the front. I'm going to check the place out. I'll signal you when I'm sure she's alone."

Phil popped the trunk and removed a small rectangular black plastic bag. "Here's the piece," he said handing him the Glock, "and a couple of extra clips. What's this other shit?"

"This shit," Marx said taking the package from Phil, "is the real safe stuff. Safe, that is until you set it off. Okay, listen up. Here's the plan. I'm going to set off an explosive on the side of the garage. When it goes off, she'll run out of there like a cockroach. Get your ass in the street in front of the house. If this broad is as savvy as I think she is, she'll have the goods with her. If she doesn't have it on her, the fire should destroy it."

"If she runs out the front door, you want me to shoot her?"

"Hell no, but if she comes out with a piece in her hand, then you'll have to take her out. Better yet, show her your badge and tell the bitch you're taking her in. I don't think she'd shoot a cop. If she resists, hold her there, I'll burn her. But remember, we've got to get the goods. Whatever you do don't go in the house. I'm going to set another bomb under the kitchen window."

"The stuff you have in the package, how can it start a fire?"

"It's an explosive. Besides, the kitchen and the laundry room should have gas appliances," Marx reminded him. "If they're in working order, then boom!"

Marx placed the package in his knapsack. He paused and looked both ways before crossing the street. He sprinted toward the warehouse dodging the stinging rain. Max stopped and glanced. He could see a woman through what looked to be the kitchen window. When he reached the warehouse, he saw that the lock on the door was broken off.

Pushing the metal door open he crossed into a spacious open area. A musty odor greeted him when he stepped inside. He squinted, letting his eyes grow accustomed to the darkness. His first impression was emptiness. The obvious firetrap was a fireman's nightmare. The pieces of broken glass hung in the windows. The place was littered with newspapers, and the floor had random puddles of water and oil. The paint-peeled black walls were lined intermittently with cardboard boxes that looked like cardboard shelter for the homeless.

Marx glanced at the ceiling. Halfway down the hallway, he thought he heard a noise behind him. He stopped and glanced over his shoulder. Was there something else in the building? Probably rats.

If there were a bum here, he wouldn't be homeless much longer. Marx would be glad to end his suffering.

He felt an uncontainable urge building inside him. He was ready to kill. He walked over to the rows of dirt and grease- smeared windows that faced the targeted house.

He pulled his knapsack from his shoulder, unzipped it then removed the package and the Colt.

Looking out the window, he muttered, "Good, the garage is attached to the side of the house."

Marx unwrapped the explosive from its black plastic cover and prepared the explosives. When he finished, he walked back outside and ducked behind the bushes between Helen's Kranski's garage and the warehouse. Max pushed aside the opening in the chain-link fence and stepped through. Looking skyward, he was glad to see the rain had suddenly diminished. The air was thick, heavy and hot. He looked up, saw the garage's roof overhang, and ducked under it. Marx placed the explosive against the side of the garage and pushed the detonator deep into the plastic charge. Staying in the soft shadows, he crouched, walking around to the side of the house, and placed another charge under the kitchen window.

He turned, looked across the street, and saw Phil sitting in the Charger.

Marx was pumped. Good, the cop's ready. He smiled. "It's show time."

*   *   *

Jake's phone went off. "Jake, it's Cohen; we just got a call from University Hospital. Detective Ferris has taken a terrible turn for the worse. He's slipped back into a coma, and they don't expect him to survive. You'd better get back here."

Jake's mind was reeling. He felt sick to his stomach.

Should he drive on to Georgetown and meet Lisa? Or should he go back to be with his dying partner?

Chapter 43

Carl Gomes crushed the Budweiser can, tossed it in the sink and said, "Three points."

Helen's eyes followed the can on its flight to the stainless steel bowl.

"Damn it, you lazy bastard," she said, reaching into her purse groping for her cigarettes. "Can't you get your fat ass up and drop that into the garbage can?"

"You do it, babe. I've got to get to get ready for my run."

The telephone went off, startling Helen.

"Hi, Lisa," Helen said. "Did you change your mind? Are you still coming?" Helen hesitated, holding her breath. "Who's coming here?" There was a pause at Helen's end. "A flash drive? What the hell is a flash drive? Hit men? A dirty cop!" She looked around the room and then went to the front window. She peered at the dark figure in the black sedan parked across from the house.

Helen's eyes flashed with anger. "Sure we've got weapons. Carl's a gun collector." There was a long pause. She finally said, "Got it, bye." She pressed the off button on the phone. "Carl, get up off your ass and get your *Benelli*. We're going to have visitors."

"Visitors? I don't like the sound of that. What kind of visitors?"

"Cops, hit men, gangsters, what the hell does it matter? I'm calling the police."

"The police?" Carl cried out, "lottsa luck, they don't like coming to this part of town."

Helen moved quickly. She twisted her blonde hair into a ponytail and tied it off. Next, she pulled off her faded red apron and took her Browning nine-millimeter from the kitchen drawer. She removed the clip, examined it, and slammed it back into the grip. Helen tried to collect her thoughts. She had to remain calm.

Carl got up from the chair and took a long look at Helen. "Cops? We didn't do anything wrong. Why do we need shotguns? They're cops."

"Cause they're not your run of the mill cops. Just get the damn thing and cover the back door."

Carl moved into the dining room as quickly as his bulk would allow. He grabbed his shotgun off the top of the wooden armoire.

The big man opened the box containing the red shells. He loaded them into the housing of the *Benelli* and headed to the back door.

Helen said, "Hey, there's someone in the backyard, and he's not wearing a badge. He's heading toward the kitchen side of the house.

That's when he spotted Marx.

"Hey, you son of a bitch, what the hell are you doing in my yard?" Carl shouted, pushing the screen door open, leveling the weapon, and firing at the intruder.

Marx dove and rolled to the right. Carl's blast missed him. Marx pressed the remote, Boom. The explosion took off the side of the garage and part of the laundry room next to the kitchen.

Marx watched the big man drop to his knees like a soiled Kleenex. Carl leveled his shotgun and took aim for another shot, but it was too late. Marx fired once hitting him in the throat. Carl wanted to fire back, but he was paralyzed. The air squeezed out of his lungs. When he began heaving for air, Marx put the second round into the big man's forehead. Carl was dead when his face hit the ground. Marx smiled quietly to himself, walked over to Carl's body, and knelt on the small of his back. He aimed at the base of the victim's skull and fired two times.

Marx's smile disappeared. Adrenaline raced through his body. His beady eyes looked wild. Red Marx was in his element. He was an assassin, he had killed before, but those were hits. In a hit, usually, the victim was unaware his life was coming to an end. This was different. To Marx, he was in the Gunfight at the O.K. Corral, and he was Wyatt Earp.

He should have kept his fat ass in the house. Now it's the bitch's turn.

* * *

Phil Westrope winced at the sound of the explosion. He got out of the Charger slowly, placed his badge in his jacket lapel, and patted his Glock.

Helen looked around, fighting rising panic. She shifted her attention to the front door. She couldn't take her eyes off the figure walking toward her. Her heart pounded.

She yanked the screen door open and walked out onto the porch. Helen kept herself in total control. She still had her nine-millimeter in her hand, wrapped in the red apron.

"What the hell are you doing?" She screamed. "Lisa called me and told me you bastards would be here. She's not coming."

"Bullshit," said Phil. He unsnapped his holster and gripped his weapon. She watched him. A sturdy, square, short man, continue to move toward the house.

"We know she was here. Just give us the flash drive she gave you, and we're gone."

Phil Westrope pulled up short.

Helen backed into the house still holding the nine-millimeter in her hand under the apron. She looked through the kitchen toward the laundry room. It was on fire.

Marx stepped into the dining room and looked at her for a moment. She knew he was sizing her up.

"Whoever you are," Marx said, "slowly, throw that apron, and whatever's in it on the floor, and move away."

Helen wrapped the apron around the Browning and slid them toward the bedroom.

"That's a good girl."

"Where's Carl?" Helen asked.

"The fat bastard is in heaven, sweetheart, or wherever bad shots go."

Helen's breath caught in her throat and then she sobbed, "You killed him, you son of a bitch!"

"Now give me the flash drive, Lisa, and I'll see to it you go free," Marx said.

"I don't know what you're talking about. My name is Helen Kranski, Lisa isn't here."

"I don't give a shit what your name is. Now if you don't stop the bullshit, and give me the flash drive, I'll blow your fucking head off too."

"Do you see this, lady?" Marx said, holding up the remote. "The rest of this place is going up like your garage. That is unless of course, you give me the flash drive."

The flames and smoke were drifting toward them. Within a few minutes, the fire would spread into the dining room.

Helen started to wail. It didn't sound human. She was beginning to sweat. Her eyes began to water. She looked over her shoulder at the open front door. A crowd was forming, and the man with the drawn pistol was flashing his gold badge, pushing them back.

"What you're looking for is in the bedroom sticking in the computer. I'll go get it," Helen said.

Marx looked at her and spoke with a soft, serious voice. "No, you won't. We'll get it together."

Helen turned and walked down the hallway with Marx close behind. She stopped when she reached the nine-millimeter wrapped in the red apron. She was standing in the doorway of the main bedroom.

"It's in there," she said pointing to the computer sitting on the desk across from the bed.

Helen hesitated at the bedroom. He tried to push her through the doorway, but she dropped to her knees. When she hit the floor, Helen picked up the apron and held it against her stomach.

Marx shook his head slightly, his eyes boring into the back of her head. "Get up and get me that flash drive!" Helen got back on her feet, and Max grabbed her by the arm and shoved her into the bedroom.

This time Helen offered no resistance. She stumbled to the computer. She took a small, plastic black pen lying beside it, and showed it to Marx.

"Good," he said, "give it to me."

Holding out the red apron draped over the nine-millimeter, Helen smiled. "Here, catch," she said, throwing the pen to Marx. Helen pointed the gun at Marx and pumped four rounds into him. He was driven back as though hit by a linebacker.

Phil, hearing the shots, reacted to his police training. He drew his piece, and raced through the front door like a dog in heat, ignoring Marx's instructions to stay outside.

Helen stepped over Marx's body into the hallway and raised the weapon. The first shot hit Phil under the left armpit. He staggered, turned, and fired his Glock. He got off one shot before it jammed. Helen fired again, and the second one hit him in the chest hurling him backward. The third ripped into his stomach.

She looked back into the room at Marx, rolling on the floor in agony. His voice distorted in pain. He smiled with blood in his teeth. Marx pushed the button on the remote control.

"To quote my brother Groucho, I've had some perfectly wonderful evenings, but this wasn't one of them."

Boom!

Jake

Chapter 44

I was left with a dilemma. Either I drive on to meet with Lisa or go back to Cincinnati to be with Sam. I couldn't help Sam, I wasn't going to pass up the chance to collar Thompson's killer.

Late April, but it felt like a day in Miami in early July. It was 3 o'clock, hot and humid, and I had a feeling that when I got to the Georgetown exit and met with Lisa, I was going to take her in, and that meant things were going to get hotter.

The AC in the unmarked wasn't doing its job. Hot beads of sweat ran a path down my cheek.

The cell in my shirt pocket went off. I checked the caller I.D. It was an area code that was becoming all too familiar: Kentucky 859.

"It's me, Jake," Lisa declared. "Where are you?"

"I'm on I-75."

"How far have you gone?"

"Far enough to know that meeting with you doesn't make sense unless of course, you're turning yourself in."

"No. I'm calling to make you a proposition."

"A proposition between you and me? That'll be the day."

"I'll ask you again, where are you?"

"I passed the Florence water tower a few minutes ago."

"When you get to the I-71 cut-off, take it towards Louisville."

"Louisville? What the hell are you up to?"

"Now's not the time to be asking questions. I'll call you again when you get to our meeting place. I'll explain everything when you get here."

"Our meeting place? Where?"

"A gas station off 71."

I was in the passing lane and somehow managed to navigate the two lanes to get me to the I-71 turnoff.

Since I was reluctant to continue our conversation, I went into defensive mode.

"You're a good talker, but you're not saying anything. Tell me right now where you are, because I'm not going on some wild goose chase. I'm turning around and going back to the hospital to be with my partner, who by the way could be dying, thanks to your friend."

"That asshole wasn't my friend. He was shooting at me too remember? Please, Jake, bear with me. It will all be over when you get here."

"Listen up, sweetheart. You're number one on my kill list. I'm tired of being ordered around by a felon. There's a rest area about a mile up the road. Unless you tell me why we're meeting, I'm not driving another mile."

"Look, Jake, I need your help," Lisa said, "You're not the only one chasing me."

"That's hardly front page news. Sam and I figured that out when we left New York. Not to mention the gunfight we had at your house. We know Joey Andronni wants a piece of you. Tell me something I don't know."

"I'm going to give it to you straight," she said. The tension in Lisa's voice told me what she was about to say something I didn't know."

"Some people in the government want me too."

I let out a long breath of air. "The government?"

"A crooked congressman from Illinois."

"Illinois, that makes sense. Honest politicians from that state are as rare as bookies forgiving your gambling debts. It's the information you saw on the flash drive, isn't it?"

I shot a glance to my right. A weigh station was coming up. Armies of eighteen-wheelers were lined up waiting to have their weight checked. The hell with the rest area, I'd stop here. I could pull into the station, park by the administration building, and focus on our conversation.

"Which congressman?"

"It doesn't matter right now. I've done some checking on you. It just so happens I think I'm going to need the services of someone who knows the law, has balls and knows what the mob is capable of. Since you have a license to practice law in Ohio, and you're a cop, you're it. Those bastards tried to kill me and would have if you hadn't been there. I liked the way you hung in against that gorilla."

"That's the second time you've said that. I'm a cop; and I want to put you behind bars, not defend you in a courtroom."

"I don't need you in a courtroom. I need your knowledge of the law."

"Get to the point," I said.

"How'd you like to get between fifteen and twenty thousand a month for the rest of your life?"

"Look, Lisa, I'm tired, and I'm pissed that we're not meeting face to face so spare me the bullshit."

"You'll be standing in money up to your neck."

Something started to take shape in my mind. Whatever I had accumulated over the years in street smarts made me suspicious. Lisa is up to something. If she needs a lawyer, whatever it is it's probably illegal.

"Who's going to give me that kind of money?" I asked.

"Your congressman friend?"

"He just might."

"He's going to put me on his re-election committee?"

"He might."

Suddenly, I was driven back to reality. "I already have a job, remember?"

"To get this lifetime payment, you're going to have to quit the force."

"Look, sweetheart, I've shoveled shit for the department in

every part of Cincinnati, and most of northern Kentucky for nine years, so don't think you can give me some cock and bull story about how you're going to set me up for the rest of my life. Turn yourself in, and I'll be in your corner."

"I can guarantee you fifteen to twenty thousand a month for the rest of your life. You can live life in the fast lane with that kind of money, can't you?"

Lisa was being very persuasive. Twenty thousand a month and all I had to do was quit the force? Leaving the force would be easy, I've always regretted not hanging a shingle, but what the hell did my ancient law degree have to do with it?

"Stay on I-71 and get off at state route 127," Lisa said. "There's a BP station on the corner. Park there and wait for my call. All your questions will be answered then. If you're smart, and I think you are, in a few weeks you'll be living like The Donald."

I pulled off 71 and hurriedly scribbled down the information she gave me.

*   *   *

Lisa pulled into the parking area in front of the BP off state route 127. She exited her car, walked into the station and asked to see the manager.

"I'm the manager," said the young man striding up to her. "What can I do for you?"

"I'd like you to give this to a Cincinnati cop who will be here in about twenty minutes," she said handing him an envelope. "His name is Jake Laird. Make sure he shows you some identification before you turn this loose."

Seeing him looking down at her cleavage, Lisa smiled and brushed her chest against the young man's biceps. "I'll be across the road watching. When he leaves, he'll wave the envelope at me so that I know you've given it to him."

Lisa pushed out her 38 double D's, winked at the smiling young man.

She blew him a kiss and slowly walked out of the store. Lisa hoped that Jake had more going for him than a cute butt, curly dark hair, and pretty blue eyes. Now, all he had to do was listen to her plan and use his legal training. If Jake was as sharp as Lisa thought he was he'd be on easy street and she'd disappear faster than spit in a hot skillet.

Chapter 45

Jake got off I-71. He parked his cruiser in the BP station and stared out across route 127.

He wondered what Lisa was up to. He admitted she looked hot, but after watching her trade bullets with Andronni's gunman he also knew she was lethal.

He sat quietly in front of the BP station for a few minutes waiting for his cell to go off. When it did, Lisa's New Jersey accent came on the line.

"Have you got my number on your speed dial?" he asked.

"Where are you?"

"Close enough."

Jake got out of the cruiser. Other than a teenager pumping gas into a dust-covered Chevy pick-up, the gas station was empty.

"You're really good at this cloak-and-dagger crap. I'm in the parking area of the BP station, and I don't see you."

"That's because you're nearsighted and I'm not anywhere near you."

Jake glanced around the empty lot and snapped, "I thought we were going to meet here."

"What do you think we're doing now? We're meeting. You didn't think I was dumb enough to let you get your hands on me, did you?"

Jake's eyes narrowed. "You're giving me a migraine. Turn yourself in now, and we'll use whatever is on that flash drive to lessen your sentence."

"No way, but as long as you're out of your car, go into the BP station. I left an envelope for you."

"What's in it?"

"You'll see when you pick it up. When you leave the station wave it outside your car window. That way, I'll know you have it."

"Then we'll meet?" Jake asked.

"No. We may never see each other again, but for now, listen. Don't interrupt me for Christ's sake, just listen."

"Okay, I'll play your game, but this better not be bullshit."

Jake entered the station, asked for the envelope, showed the man his identification, and returned to his car. He looked around, held it high, and waved it as she had instructed.

Lisa was back on Jake's cell.

"I see you have the envelope, but don't open it yet."

"Look, I'm totally pissed right now, so stop playing games with me."

"This is no game, Jake," Lisa said. "If you don't like the proposition, then keep chasing me, but I can tell you like Jimmy Hoffa, I'm going to disappear."

Jake considered Lisa's comment for a moment.

"What makes you think I want anything to do with you, but to turn you in?"

Lisa said, "Hear me out, there's no harm in listening."

"Lady, there's always harm in listening."

"I can see you from here, your halo is beginning to slip."

Jake ignored the remark and Lisa continued explaining my part of the plan.

"Do what? All those cities? I can't do that. I'm a police officer, remember?"

"You're also an attorney. If you quit the force and then do it, is it legal?"

He thought for a minute. If he resigned, Jake wouldn't be working for the city. What she was proposing was illegal, for her, but not for him. He remained silent. It did sound intriguing. She had got him to come this far. He might as well listen to the rest of her proposal.

"I suppose it's legal, but the devil is in the details."

Lisa continued. "Setting this up will make you be a world traveler."

Jake marveled at her ability to talk so dispassionately about something that was so hazardous. This was one tough lady.

"One more question, Lisa, you want me to meet with these people? If I fool with Andronni I could get my head blown off."

"No, you won't meet them face to face."

"Whatever you're planning, they're not going to take this lying down."

"Yes they are," she said, "we've got them over a barrel."

"What's this we shit? There's no limit to what they can do, separately or together. The only barrel we're going to see is the one they put us in before they drop us in the Ohio River."

"Believe me, Jake, there's enough information on the flash drive to send congressman Morrison and Andronni away for a long time."

"Morrison? The senator from Illinois?"

There was a moment of silence.

"One and the same."

"I don't know, lady, this sounds dangerous."

"You can handle danger. I saw you in action at my place. That's why I picked you. Think about it. I'll get back to you."

The blood-red orange sun was descending as Jake sat in the cruiser thinking about Lisa's offer.

He didn't fully understand why she picked him. He knew the law and the way mobsters thought. The gunfight at her place made him sympathetic to her plight. He was getting tired of chasing criminals only to have them go free with the help of some crafty lawyer.

The way Lisa made it sound this deal could set him up for life. The question was would he have the balls to pull it off?

*   *   *

Jake was about to leave when his cell went off again, but this time the area code read 513.

"Detective Laird, Commander Cohen, here. There's been an unfortunate incident in Nashville. It looks like our killer blew herself to hell rather than be taken in."

I had to go along with their theory. I knew it wasn't Lisa, but this wasn't the time to let Cohen know.

"She blew herself up?"

"I'm afraid so, and she took Lieutenant Westrope with her."

"Oh my God," Jake exclaimed, "When did this happen?"

"About an hour ago. The fire department brought the fire under control. Three bodies were removed from the house, Westrope an unidentified male, and a female. We think the female was Lisa Turnbull, but that hasn't been confirmed. There was also a male found in the back of the house with gunshot wounds."

"So you're not sure it was her."

"Only Westrope was ID'd for sure. His cruiser, with Hamilton County plates on it, was parked across from the house, so we're pretty sure one of the bodies was his. The male, in the back of the house, was ID'd by the next door neighbor."

"What about Sam? Have you heard anything more from the hospital?"

"Yes, Jake, I hope you're sitting down. We've lost two of Cincinnati's finest today. Your partner slipped back into a coma and passed away."

Jake

Chapter 46

The news of Sam's death tore me apart inside. I was ready to cry or scream. Now that Sam is gone, partner is the most important word in my vocabulary.

According to The American College Dictionary, the word is defined as a sharer or partaker, an associate, one's companion. Sam was more than all of those. He was special.

I've got a dictionary at home my dad bought me in the late sixties. Back then, gay meant having or showing a joyous mood. It didn't become a word associated with homosexuals until the late eighties. At least it didn't work for me. Like every other teenager, I made fun of the word and the people we attached the phrase gay too.

Sam and I would argue about the use of the word partner. It started in different ways but always ended up the same. I was a homophobe or behind the times.

I've done a lot of dumb things in my life, and if I listed them in order, not understanding the true meaning of Sam's companionship is right at the top of the list.

When I referred to Sam as my partner, the other detectives would smile and snicker.

I can remember when Lieutenant Westrope told me I was getting a new partner. He clued the detectives in vice squad first before he told me and that naturally led to the teasing.

Detective Collins asked, "What do you do if you and your partner are taking a shower at the same time and your partner drops the soap?"

"Nothing," his partner answered. "Don't worry, Jake, as long as you don't feel two hands on your shoulders, you'll be okay."

Both those clowns backed off when they met Sam.

Funny, they never teased me about Sam being my partner while he was within earshot, but when he wasn't around, it was time to pull my chain and watch me squirm.

Now, all I could think of was my reaction to what Dr. Bennett the day Sam was gunned down.

"It's touch and go, you'd better call his family."

Sam was gay and never hid it. When he checked into the department, he was already out of the closet. He wore his gay lifestyle like a badge of courage.

The way I look at it, he took a slug for me. He didn't have to come in blasting. Like on our first patrol together, his partner was in a firefight, and he was there for me.

If I have had the right attitude and stood up to those assholes in the division, they would have stopped.

I laughed at it all, and so did Sam, but I know he felt sorry for me. Sam was my partner. I wish my partner were here now, taking a shower with me. I'd drop the soap, and I'd be happy to hesitate before picking it up.

Jake

CHAPTER 47

I can't believe this. Half of me was gone, the fun half. This job was tough enough, but without Sam's humor, and loyalty, I doubt I could have lasted on the job this long.

I rolled the window back up and pulled out of the BP station. Sam was like a brother to me. There's a special bond that develops between detectives who are assigned to work together. You have to know that the other guy is always watching your back. After five years together, Sam and I had begun to think like one. He was someone I could trust. It had been a long, hard time since I put my complete trust in a partner. I don't think I can work with anyone but Sam. His killer is dead, but not that son-of-a-bitch Andronni.

I started to think about Lisa's proposal and the part Andronni, and his congressman played in it. With Lisa's deal, I could pay the bastards back and carry it out from anywhere in the world. If I stayed on the force, I'd have to break in a new partner. None of them would be anything like Sam. What if my new partner turned out to be a kiss ass kind of guy? What if he was more interested in PC than going after the bad guys? What if I had to partner up with a woman?

My cell went off again. Area code 513, this time it was Veronica's number.

"Jake? It's me, Veronica, I just heard about Sam. I'm so sorry."

"Cohen called, he told me. I don't understand. I left Sam this morning. He looked like he was getting better."

"Just because he looked like he was on the mend, doesn't mean he was. That's why he was in ICU."

"What happened?"

"He had an aneurysm. I'm surprised it wasn't picked up, earlier, but it probably was too small. Suddenly, his blood pressure dropped, and his heart rate went through the roof. He had a stroke, and he slipped into a coma. They tried to get him into the operating room, but he died on the way. He never regained consciousness. I'm going over to University Hospital now. Where are you?"

"On 71, I should be back in town," I looked at the clock on the dashboard, "about four."

"Meet me in my office. I'm going to have Sam brought here rather than a mortuary. Oh, by the way, I just heard Phil Westrope died in an explosion in Nashville."

"I know. The bastard had it coming."

"Jake! I know you didn't like him, but he was a cop."

"Yeah, a dirty one, the son-of-a-bitch is the reason Sam is dead. I'll explain that later when I get back, but right now I'm going to Commander Cohen's office."

*   *   *

I called Cohen back and asked him not to leave the office until I got to town. I had a lot to think about on the drive back to Cincinnati. Westrope was the dirty cop. I had to tell Cohen I knew the woman who died in the Nashville explosion wasn't Lisa. How was I going to tell him Thompson's killer was still on the loose?

Without Sam, and my retirement, Lisa's deal started to sound plausible. I had been on the force for twenty years, so I was eligible for a pension. What the hell was I thinking? If I teamed up with Lisa, I wouldn't need a pension. The package and its contents would answer all my questions.

Driving over the Ohio River, my cell went off again. It was that damn Lisa again.

"Well Jake, have you thought it over?" she asked.

"No, I haven't. I haven't had the time to look at what's in it. It looks like your skipping Nashville saved your life. Our people think you blew yourself up rather than be taken in. They have a female body, but sooner or later they're going to find out it's not yours."

"Helen," Lisa said softly, "I tried to warn her. I called her. I told her your people were on the way there."

"Why would she blow herself up?" I asked.

"That doesn't make sense, she wouldn't do that. She told me she had guns, but Helen wouldn't use them unless she was fired upon. Knowing her, they must have forced her into a firefight."

"They also found three other bodies," I went on. "One was the Cincinnati cop who drove my partner's killer to your place. Another male was identified as having lived there."

"What about the third?" She asked.

"He's still a mystery."

"If he was with a dirty cop, your mystery's solved. He's probably a hitter from Chicago or South Beach. My guess it was one of the Marx brothers. Rumor has it that they got on Andronni's hitter's list when I didn't fulfill my contract. Take a look at my proposition, but hurry, times a wasting."

"Back down lady, you just asked me twenty minutes ago."

"Well, I wish you'd think about it, and you better think fast. If it was one of the Marx brothers, you're on their list too. They were three of them. You can bet your ass," she added, "the contract on you will be given to one of them."

I heard a click.

Jake

Chapter 48

Commander Cohn was waiting for me at the door of his office when I arrived at District 1.

I walked through a group of uniformed officers and clerks, patting me on the back, and giving me condolences for Sam. Cohen called out my name loudly and waved me over to him.

Commander Cohen stepped between the men, put his arm around me and led me into his office. That certainly was unusual. There was always coldness about Cohen. He pointed to the stuffed chair opposite his desk and I dropped into it.

Cohen swung around and pointed to the seal of Cincinnati on the wall behind his desk.

"Detective Sam Ferris and Lieutenant Phil Westrope gave their lives in the line of duty for this great full city. We're going to honor them."

I shook my head. A part of me wanted to let the whole thing burst out about Phil. I didn't want the son-of-a bitch's name mentioned in the same breath with Sam's.

"I just got off the phone with the mayor and he wants to hold a memorial service for the two slain officers."

"No, we're not," I replied. "Sir, Sam's death was in the line of duty, Phil's was in the line of bullshit. He was the mole, and our killer is still loose."

Cohen put his knuckles on his desk and leaned toward me. His face turned red with anger as he rose to his feet. He looked around the office as if there might be someone else in the room.

"Did you just pull that shit out of your ass, Detective Laird? Phil has been my right hand for the past three years. I think I'd have known if he was dirty."

"Commander, it wouldn't be the first time you were wrong about a guy."

Cohn sat back down and placed his hands on his desk to calm himself. "Where'd you get this, Laird?"

"Lisa Turnbull told me she had a contract to hit our guy in The Royal Cincinnatian for the mob."

Cohen's face tightened. "What!" He exclaimed. "You've been talking to our suspect?"

I sighed. "Yeah, the woman found in the fire in Nashville is not our killer. Ours is still on the loose. She told me the other male body you found was a probably a hitter named Marx. Being with Marx finally brought Westrope out of the shadows."

Cohen sighed uncomfortably. "When did this conversation take place?"

"This afternoon. Just after you called me and told me about Sam."

"She told you Phil Westrope was working for the mob? And you believed her?"

"Yes."

His eyes were boring into mine. "And you think she's creditable?"

"Yes, sir, I do. There's a link between Phil and those bastards from New York. They've been one step ahead of Sam and me since we were assigned this case."

"You're going to have more than our suspect's word before I can act on this information."

"Sergeant Cullen, at the motor pool, told me Phil Westrope was the guy who drove your cruiser with Joey Andronni's men to Lisa's house. It all adds up, it had to be that bastard, Phil."

Cohen came from behind his desk, walked over to the large window on the other side of the office, and instinctively closed the blinds.

"Who else knows this detective?"

A fire was building up inside of me. I had to get out of his office. I started to get up, but he motioned me back down. I hesitated. I was too tired to argue, but I was faced with an unsettling choice. I already mentioned Cullen, but not Lopez.

"The killer, Sergeant Cullen, me," I said, looking into his eyes, hoping to see a reaction, "and now," I paused, "you."

He shook his head and smiled thinly. "The mayor wants a memorial. It wouldn't be in his or the department's interest for this to get out, now would it?"

"That's because it's an election year, and right now, I really don't give a damn about the mayor's re-election, sir. Phil Westrope was responsible for Sam's death and I'm not honoring his ass, and neither should the department."

"I'm going to ignore that remark, detective Laird. With your involvement in this case, the death of your partner and all, I know you've been under a lot of pressure. I think you'd better take some time off and think about it. It might help you see things differently."

I turned to leave, but I could see Cohen wasn't finished talking. This meeting was over. He grabbed me by the arm, stepped up, and got in my face.

"This needs to be kept in this office, detective."

My adrenaline began to flow. I couldn't believe what he had just said. I stood there staring at him, that's when I made a fist and slammed it down on Cohen's desk.

"I'll make a deal with you, sir. Sam gets the memorial service and my lips are sealed. Include Phil in whatever you're planning and I'll open up a shit storm you'll never get out from under."

*   *   *

My meeting with Cohen pushed me over the edge. The thought of having a contract on me was unnerving. I called Veronica and left her a message that I wasn't going to meet her in her office. I was going to have to tell her that after twenty-one years on the force I was going to hand in my resignation. I was going home and get shit-faced in honor of my fallen partner. I made up my mind. With

Sam gone, I was gone too.

Driving home I kept hearing what sounded like Sam's voice. It kept repeating, "take the deal, Tracy, it's perfect for us."

Sam was the only one who ever referred to me as Tracy.

When I got back to my place, I let Maggie in through the back door and headed for the fridge. I took a bottle of vodka out of the freezer, plopped down on the sofa. I poured myself a drink to celebrate my decision to leave the force and cry over the loss of Sam.

I hit the play button on my answering machine. There were two calls. One was from Veronica. She got my message and asked me to call her when I got home. The other was from Herman Williamson, the Cincinnati Enquirer reporter who met me at the hospital when Sam was shot. He wanted to interview me about Sam's death and the investigation. I'd call Veronica back, but I was in no mood to talk to a reporter about my fallen partner or the case.

I got up, went into the kitchen, and fixed myself a ham and cheese sandwich. I was out of beer so I guess I'll have to wash it down with the vodka.

I opened Lisa's envelope and pulled out its contents.

She was right about one thing the plan she had laid out was as simple as it was brilliant. It was fool proof, but, risky, rash, and dangerous. Her part in it was definitely illegal, but probably not mine. I don't know why she thinks she needs a lawyer. I'd have to crack a few of my old law books to be sure. One thing was certain leaving the force had to happen before I entered into any partnership with Lisa. I've got to admit, I like a woman who colors outside the lines.

But should Lisa go scot-free? She killed an accountant who was hiding illegal transactions between a congressman and a mobster. Thompson was Morrison's man. Andronni wanted his own guy. A guy he could trust. It was becoming obvious that if Lisa wanted to disappear she would. Without Sam, hanging a shingle should be the next step in my life.

Her plan was stunning in its simplicity. According to what she had laid out, all we had to do was trust each other.

It was about time I saw what was on the thing that cause the deaths of eight people and my partner Sam.

I placed the flash drive into my laptop. When the screen lit up I could see several icons. The first one was labeled, International Service Workers Union Funds, a Thailand operation and two others that read Morrison and Andronni.

I paused, if I looked at this information, Lisa and I would have something in common. We'd both be on Andronni and Morrison's hit list.

Oh, what the hell. What else did have to do now that I'm going to retire? This could be fun.

Jake

Chapter 49

The phone rang four times. "Senator Morrison."

His voice was deep and polished. He was a man enjoying its sound.

"It all depends on who this is. Where'd you get this number?"

"Never mind, I got it and don't want to spend a whole lot of time talking to you, senator. I've got a piece of plastic you and Joey have been trying to get your hands on."

"I'll ask you again, who are you?"

"I'm the guy that's got you by the short, curly ones. Now listen closely. I don't want to repeat myself."

I ran Lisa's plan by him, but I don't think he was impressed.

"This must be some kind of a joke. Who do you think you are?"

"I'm the voice of your hitter. I'm the one who's going to make sure you keep your end of the bargain."

"My hitter? I don't know what you're talking about. This is nonsense. You can't do that. That's against the law."

"Whose law senator? The laws you make or the ones you break?"

"Do you think Andronni and I are idiots? How do we know what's on that flash drive will harm us?"

"A special courier will drop it off at your home in Georgetown this evening. Don't fool with the kid who delivers it. He was given money to deliver the package and has no idea who gave it to him or what's in it. Look at it, if it doesn't concern you, you're home free."

"Have you seen what's on it?"

I sighed. "Yes, I did. You've been a busy boy, senator. Getting contributions from foreign counties, and having mobsters funnel union money to help finance your campaign. I think that's a no-no. The senate ethics committee would like to see it."

"Who the hell do you think you're talking to? I grew up on the south side of Chicago. We invented intimidation."

This guy sounds like a thug. He was wearing out my patience

"I'll be sure to tell Andronni you're not interested in his welfare."

"That's not what I meant."

I let my voice drop. "I know what you meant, senator. Look at the flash drive, make up your mind, and then go back to protecting your ass."

There was a slight pause. "How do I know you'll keep them away from the press?"

"You don't, but if you do as the lady says, you're home free. Let me correct that. You'll be home, but it won't be free."

*   *   *

Joey 'the priest' Andronni was another story. I had to get by someone who answered to Paulie and he didn't sound too friendly

I heard him call out, "It's some shyster and he says it's in your best interest to take this call."

I could hear Andronni all the way from Miami, which was where I was at the time.

Paulie got back on the phone. "He says he doesn't talk to ambulance chasers."

"Tell your boss I've got a message from the woman he contracted to hit his accountant, Hank Thompson."

Paulie raised his voice. "Where'd you get this number?"

"Out of your ass, bozo. Tell your boss the goods his hitter took from Thompson is going to Sean Hannity and Fox News if he doesn't come to the phone, now."

"Who the fuck are they?"

"The cable television station."

Paulie called out. "The shyster says he's got something you want from Thompson's hitter."

That brought Joey Andronni grumbling to the phone, and the war of words were about to begin.

"Where's my property, friend?" Andronni asked.

"What property?"

"Don't be a wise ass. You know what property, the flash drive."

I could see this was going to be fun.

"I'm not your friend, Mr. Andronni. What I meant was which flash drive are you referring to?"

Andronni said, "If you're calling me you know what I'm talking about."

"You'll get it, but it's going to cost you."

"I thought so, friend. What if I turn this over to my lawyers? Maybe you've heard of them? Glock, Remington and Glock."

"Look, I don't want to spend too much time talking to you. I had to run this by your partner, Senator Morrison three times. He's not as savvy as you are, so I know you'll get it the first time. You see there are eight flash drives. Your friend in Washington has one. You're about to get one, and the other six are spread around the world."

"Look friend, we're going to get our hands on this broad and my guess is she can't talk under water. After we do her it will be your turn. When we find you, we'll cut off your balls and stuff them down your throat."

"You're making me crap my pants here, Joey. Copies of what your accountant had in his computer are in Chicago, London, Berlin, Rome, Zurich, Los Angeles, of course the one with your partner in Washington."

"That's seven my friend, where's the eighth?"

I was impressed; this gangster knew how to add.

"If you're in Little Italy, it's probably right under your guinea nose."

"Tell me, wise ass, how much is it going to cost me to keep these six copies under lock and key?"

"You are smarter than your Senator friend. Each of you will send twenty thousand a month to an account in Zurich,

Switzerland. The account number of the institution will be in the package you get with your copy of the flash drive."

"And what if I don't go for this blackmail bullshit?"

"Funny Joey, your friend in Washington asked the same question."

"And?"

"We'll turn loose all six of them," I replied.

"And what if one of us misses a payment?"

"Then the other one will have to send in forty K."

"Tell me, shyster, why am I talking to you and not my hitter?"

"I'm her safety valve. Your hitter and I will be in touch with each other weekly. If anything happens to either one of, like my balls ending up down my throat or she's found floating in the Ohio River, all six remaining flash drives will be distributed to the press."

"What happens if one of you gets hit by a car or struck by lighting?"

"The other one sends all of the flash drives to the media."

"And one of you dies of natural causes?"

"Ditto, so you better pray we stay healthy."

"That's a lot of money, friend. What if I tell you to go fuck yourself?"

"I don't think you'll do that, Joey. The way I figure it twenty K is one week's take of your drug business in Harlem."

"And the guy in Washington?" Andronni asked. "What if he tells you to take a hike?"

"He didn't, Morrison's on board. He wants to run for president, remember. That's chump change to him. He's from Chicago they invented stealing from each other, it's the Chicago way. I'm sure he'll find a way to get his party to pick up the tab. If we play ball together, your hitter will be made comfortable and you both will remain hidden."

"How do I know we can trust your ass?"

"You don't. Let's just say it's in our best interest to trust one another."

"You haven't heard the end of me, friend."

"I told you, I'm not your friend. I suggest you cancel the

contract you gave to the Marx brothers to have me disappear. You want to drop the contract on her too. If you don't do this Joey, it will make a great story on the evening news."

I hung up smiling. At this moment I've never been as excited as I was in 1976 when the Cincinnati Reds, swept the New York Yankees, in the World Series.

* * *

When I got back to the hotel in South Beach Veronica was waiting for me.

"How'd your meeting go?" she asked.

"We've got a problem. We can't go back to Cincinnati just yet. I have to drop some things off for a client."

"Where're we going?" she said with a sparkle in her eye.

"I've got work to do in Switzerland. Then it's off to London, Rome, and a for a week of R and R in Monte Carlo."

There goes that voice in the back of my head again.

"You messed up, Jake. Some lover you are. You're going to Europe with a beautiful woman, and you're not going to take her to Paris for an evening on the River Seine? Boy, am I glad you're not gay. If you were, you'd be giving us a bad name."

"You're right Catchem."

"Veronica," I asked. "Have you ever seen the Eiffel Tower up close?"

NOTES